RAY OF LOVE

(Ray Series #3)

E. L. TODD

Fallen Publishing

Ray of Love

Editing Services provided by Final-Edits.com

Chapter One

Three Months Later...

Rae

I didn't realize I was over Ryker until I stopped thinking about him. But I didn't realize I had stopped thinking about him because I wasn't thinking about him. When I thought about him for the first time in seven days, I realized he wasn't on my mind anymore.

I was finally free.

It was a dark three months. I put on a brave face for everyone else, but my nights were lonely, and the time I spent alone in the lab was the most difficult. I had flashbacks of our romance, of our nights together and all the great times we had. Overwhelming loss would hit me hard in the chest when I least expected it.

But then I remembered I had no reason to miss him.

He didn't deserve me, and I needed to forget about Ryker and find someone who did.

I walked into the kitchen and saw Rex sitting at the table. He always looked like a train wreck in the morning because he stayed out too late the night before. He went out with some girl and didn't come back until some obscene hour. I didn't ask about the details because I'd have rather not known.

I poured a mug of coffee and made a bowl of cereal. "Still alive over there?"

Rex rested his face in his hands as he stared down into his coffee, one eye open. "Uh-huh."

"Want some cereal?"

"Nah…" He yawned loudly then rubbed the sleep from his eye.

I took a seat at the table and enjoyed my breakfast before I had to head off to work. I stayed at COLLECT because I loved my job and refused to move just because Ryker ran the show. As long as he didn't come downstairs for a visit, there was no reason for us to see each other. The only interaction I had with him was looking at his signature on my checks. "If you hate waking up early, why do you go to work in the morning?"

"I've got to take care of all the office stuff. You wouldn't understand."

"That's right." I narrowed my eyes. "Because I'm stupid…"

"Exactly."

A knock sounded on the front door.

Who would be there that early before work? "Come in."

Zeke opened the door and walked inside, wearing his dark blue scrubs before he headed off to work. Even in baggy clothes, the muscles of his body were noticeable. His face was cleanly shaven, and his hair looked nice. "Hey." A newspaper was tucked under his arm, and he didn't seem as cheerful as he usually was.

"Something up?" Rex asked.

"Yeah…" Zeke took a seat at the head of the table and opened the paper until he reached the obituary section. "Rae, I'm sorry to tell you this. I know you were fond of him." He turned the paper and showed me the article. "I didn't want you to walk into work without knowing."

"What is it?" I pulled the paper closer to me and realized Mr. Price had passed away. "Oh no..." I set my mug on the table and read the article from beginning to end. It said he had a short battle with cancer before he lost the fight. He was survived by two sons.

I guess Ryker did have a brother.

Zeke watched me, studying my face for signs of distress.

"That's..." There were no words to describe what I was feeling. Mr. Price was always so nice to me and to everyone who worked at COLLECT. He had a generous spirit and a heart that could love everyone in every single room he stepped into. "That's so terrible." I read the remaining paragraphs. "It says Ryker took over when he was first diagnosed so he could spend the last few months of his life with his family..." Now Ryker's attitude made sense. He really was forced to take the job.

"So sad," Zeke said. "I know you were fond of him."

"I was..." Once the initial shock wore off, I thought of my ex. "I hope Ryker is okay. This must be hard for him..." I remembered the tense conversations we had about his family. He asked me to never discuss his father, and now it made sense. Ryker knew he was dying of cancer, and it was just too hard to talk about.

"Who gives a shit?" Rex snapped.

"Rex." I set down the paper and gave him a cold look. "There's no need to be vicious like that."

"Like I give a damn." He drank his coffee and didn't remove his hateful scowl. "It's not like I knew the old man anyway."

"It's still not okay." Despite what Ryker did to me, he didn't deserve to go through this. No one should have to bear the pain of losing a parent.

5

Fortunately, Zeke was on my side for this one. "The funeral is tomorrow."

"Please don't tell me you're going to go," Rex snapped. "Because that bitch face will be there."

"Of course I'm going to pay my respects to Mr. Price. And I don't care if Ryker is there. If anything...I'd like to tell him I'm sorry for his loss." We'd been broken up long enough that we could be civil to one another. In times of tragedy, petty differences should be put aside. And when I said I loved him three months ago, I meant it. I didn't feel that way anymore, but I could never be so cold to someone I ever felt that way about.

"He doesn't deserve your pity," Rex said. "I'm not going."

"You are," I said firmly.

"Fuck. No." He leaned back in his chair and gave me that typical attitude.

"He's your friend, Rex. Yours too, Zeke." Our breakup shouldn't tear them apart.

6

"He stopped being my friend the second he fucked you over," Rex said.

"Me too," Zeke said. "I'm sorry, Rae. But what he did wasn't cool."

"Well, will you please go to the funeral for me?" I looked them both in the eye. "Because I would like it if you were there."

Zeke's eyes immediately softened. "Okay."

Since Zeke gave in, Rex felt obligated to as well. "Fine. Whatever."

***

After the ceremony in the church, we arrived at the gravesite. They placed the coffin next to the newly dug grave. It was rich mahogany, the dark wood designed and made for a king. It was the most beautiful coffin I'd ever seen, as morbid a thought as it was.

People gathered around to say their goodbyes. Quietly, guests left so they could attend the wake being held at the Four Seasons in Seattle. The three of us weren't planning on attending the service because I worried our extended presence may make Ryker feel uncomfortable. All I really wanted to do was say goodbye.

I spotted Ryker alongside his mother. She wore all black with a veil covering her face. She was crying, weeping openly for the man she lost. She was tall, just like her son. Even though her face was mostly hidden, I could tell she was pretty.

She cried into Ryker's shoulder as he hugged her waist, supporting his mom during this difficult time. He wore the same cold expression he always had, his thoughts and emotions impossible to read.

A man I could only assume was his brother came to their mother's side and consoled her next. He wrapped his arm around her shoulder and guided her to speak to someone who approached the grave.

Ryker remained where he was, staring at the coffin where his father lay.

I stared at him and felt intense pain wash over me. Even though he didn't wear his heart on his sleeve, I knew he was crying a river inside. I knew he was suffering a battle no one could see. He was devastated, even if he refused to show it.

"Let's go pay our respects." I walked around the grave until I approached Ryker from the side, Zeke and Rex trailing behind me.

When Ryker looked up, he clearly wasn't expecting to me. His eyes dilated like I shined a light in them. His expression was unreadable, but I knew he felt something when he saw me. It was the first time we'd looked at each other since I told him off outside that bar.

I stopped when I was directly in front of him, but I was still an arm's length away. The last thing I wanted him to think was that this was a confrontation. "I'm so sorry, Ryker..." I wanted to hug him, even shake his hand. But I didn't think affection would be permitted based on where our relationship stood. "Your dad was a great man. We'll all miss him."

He stared at me like he wasn't sure I was real.

I couldn't tell if my words were welcome or not. I stepped to the side so the guys could speak to him.

Zeke extended his hand and shook Ryker's. "I'm sorry for your loss."

Ryker nodded in gratitude.

Rex came next, but he faltered in discomfort. It churned his insides to be the bigger man when it came to Ryker. He would never forgive him for what he did to me. Rex was far too protective of me to let it go.

But finally, he found the grace to be civil. He shook his head. "I'm sorry, Ryker." That was all he could force himself to say.

Ryker nodded again.

Rex walked away and joined Zeke. There was nothing else to say. It was time to leave so Ryker could be alone to grieve. We turned away and headed back to our car.

"Rae." It was the first time Ryker spoke, and his voice was deeper than it'd ever been before.

We all stopped and turned around.

Ryker turned away from the grave and stared at me, waiting for me to come back to his side.

Rex gave me a look that said I should keep walking.

Zeke didn't have a reaction.

I crossed the wet grass until we were face-to-face again. I saw the heartbreak in Ryker's blue eyes. I saw the whirlwind of pain. My bitterness toward him finally disappeared when I realized my pain over our breakup was nothing in comparison to what he felt right now.

"I'm sorry for everything that happened between us. I want you to know that."

The last thing I expected was an apology—at least on a day like this. "It's okay, Ryker. I've forgiven you and moved on with my life." It felt so good to say that, to say I was okay and actually mean it. "I hope you find peace." I reached up and touched his arm, letting my hand rest there for several heartbeats. I felt the warmth burn from his body. And I also felt him shake slightly. "Take care."

***

"I think you did the right thing, Rae." Zeke walked beside me down the hallway. Rex was up ahead, walking faster than both of us because he was starving. He got the apartment door unlocked and darted inside.

"Yeah?" I pulled my jacket closer around my body to fight the chill.

"I mean...I was really angry about the whole thing. The way he treated you...not cool. But I think the fact that you're so mature and forgiving about it probably makes him feel worse, in a way."

"How?"

"It makes him realize the diamond he truly lost." Zeke nudged me in the side and gave me a smile.

"Maybe. But I doubt he's thinking about anything like that right now."

"Probably not. But I bet he wishes you were beside him during this difficult time."

I snorted because Zeke was dead wrong about that. "We were dating when his father had cancer, and he never told me about it. He's never wanted me to be there for him."

"Maybe he does now."

I had a greater probability of winning the lottery. "Thanks for coming today."

"No big deal. Ryker and I used to be friends. I think it was good Rex and I were there."

"Me too."

We walked into the apartment just as Rex was walking out.

"Where are you going?"

He was still chewing something because he stuffed his face in less than thirty seconds before he took off again. "Gunea mucha."

I cocked my head to the side in confusion. "What?"

Rex tried again. "Ginea deeata."

"Rex!" I threw my arms down. "Swallow and then talk!"

"I got it," Zeke said. "He said he has a date."

Rex gave him a thumbs-up before he walked off.

I turned back to Zeke. "How the hell did you figure that out?"

Zeke shrugged. "Being best friends since we were five. That's how." He walked into my apartment and snatched a beer from the fridge. "I got the whole day off from work, so you wanna do something?"

"Does that mean your office is closed?"

"No. If I closed it down, people would lose a day of work. Some of my employees might like having the day off, but I know others need those hours to pay bills and what not."

"So...they're running a practice without a doctor?"

"No." He chuckled then sat at the kitchen table. "I have a friend filling in for me."

"That's cool. At least you have someone to take over for you when you're sick." It was too early in the day for beer, so I grabbed a water and sat across from him.

Zeke sipped his beer and stared at me. His blue eyes narrowed slightly as he took me in, their brilliance not as obvious as less light entered them. Something serious was coming. It was only a matter of time before he spit it out. "So...how was it seeing him for the first time?" His fingers rested around his glass as it sat on the table.

"Um...I don't know." I knew I would see Ryker again somewhere down the road. If Zeke had asked me that a few months ago, I would have had a much

15

different reaction. I wouldn't have been able to stop myself from daydreaming about Ryker wanting me to take him back. But now it was different.

"You don't know?"

"Getting over him was really hard for me. I know I put on a brave face for everyone, but it really was a struggle."

His eyes softened.

"And when you love someone once, you kinda always love them, you know?" I knew that didn't make any sense. "I don't have feelings for him anymore, but I definitely don't want him to ever be in pain. I guess I'll always care about him in some way."

He nodded. "I understand that."

"When I looked at him, I didn't feel any of the things I used to feel. But I definitely felt his pain."

He nodded again.

"I'm not sure when I finally got over him. I think it was probably a few weeks ago. I stopped thinking about him altogether. I stopped wondering who he was bringing back to his apartment. I just...stopped caring."

"That's good. It takes a while to get there, but you made it." He clanked his bottle against my glass. "And now you're free."

"Yeah, I guess so."

"So you're going to jump back into the dating pool?"

The idea was repulsive. "Absolutely not."

"Really?" Both of his eyebrows rose. "Jump back on the horse."

"I don't have any urge to. I guess I'm over the dating scene. The only type of guys I go for are assholes." I was drawn to them like a moth to a flame. Their inability to commit was desirable, and their coldness just drew me in even more. I considered myself to be a smart woman, but that clearly only applied to textbooks.

"You've kissed some frogs, but you'll find your Prince Charming, Rae. Don't worry about that."

"I've never really cared about settling down before, but now I really want it. I want to find my husband, someone who truly loves me and doesn't play games, and I just want to be happy." I stared down into my water glass and only felt a little uncomfortable making that confession to Zeke. But since he was my best friend, he would understand. "I know that makes me sound like—"

"It doesn't." He gave me the same fond look he always used to give me. "Not at all. You're just finally at that place where you're ready for the real thing. Now you understand how much you want it."

"When did that happen for you?"

He narrowed his eyes like he didn't know what I was asking.

"It seems like you're pretty serious with Rochelle. I just assumed you considered settling down once you met."

"Oh...yeah. I guess I got tired of sleeping around. Rex and I had shared a few girls a while ago, and while it was adventurous and exciting, I realized just how lonely I really was."

Instead of being disgusted by what he said about my brother, I focused on what he said about himself. And I actually felt bad for him.

"It made me feel empty. I had nothing more important in my life than fucking around. It made me realize I wanted a woman who was more exciting than any three or foursome I could possibly have. I have my house and my practice, and now I want a beautiful wife to share that with. I want to have kids. I guess I'm ready to move forward—like you."

"And you see that with Rochelle?"

He looked down at his beer before he took a drink. "Yeah...I think so."

"Well, good for you. It looks like your search is over." And mine was only beginning. "I like Rochelle because she's classy, you know? She's fun to be around, but she also has that elegance that automatically makes you respect her. I think she'd be a great woman to share your life with."

He took a long drink of his beer until it was completely empty. When he set it on the table, it made a distinctive tap. "I'm glad you guys like her…"

"She's definitely my favorite in comparison to the others you've brought around." I realized how rude I sounded, so I quickly tried to rectify it. "Not that there was anything wrong with them, I just—"

"It's okay," he said with a chuckle. "I know what you mean."

An awkward moment hung between us, a pregnant silence filled with words unsaid. I looked out the window because I didn't know what else to do. It was the only time I felt uncomfortable around Zeke, even though I couldn't explain why.

"You want to get lunch at Mega Shake?" he asked.

I'd never say no to Mega Shake. "That sounds like a great idea."

***

I watched him eat a double-double and two orders of fries—all by himself. "Damn, you were hungry."

"I skipped breakfast, and I hit the gym hard yesterday. Haven't had any recovery food." He placed a handful of fries into his mouth and chewed them quicker than Rex ever did. "I swear, I don't normally eat like a pig."

"I don't think you're a pig," I said. "I'm impressed."

He laughed. "I don't think most women would be."

"Dude, if I ate that much, my thighs would explode."

He rolled his eyes. "Rae, you have beautiful legs. Shut up."

"I didn't say anything about my legs. Just my thighs. All the fat goes to my thighs—every time."

"That's pretty typical for women. In men, it goes to their stomachs."

I eyed the top part of his stomach over the table. "Then where does yours go?"

"To the gym," he said with a smile. "Weightlifting boosts your metabolism and helps you burn fat all day long."

"I'm not much of a lifter. I like to run, but that's about it. And unless I'm chasing after a ball, I'm pretty bored."

He chuckled. "That makes sense. I don't do enough cardio, so maybe we should play ball together every day."

"One on one?"

"Yeah."

"Well, if you want to get your ass kicked every day, that's fine by me."

"Here comes the shit talk..."

"I'm not shit talking. I'm just giving you a heads-up."

22

"Rae, I'm not worried about it. I'm pretty sure we'd be competitive adversaries. And we'd get a serious workout."

"I don't know... It's one thing to lose to a woman once, but over and over? That might get old."

He shoved a few more fries into his mouth. "You're cocky, aren't you?"

"Hey, you've seen me on the court."

"Well, maybe you need to get a reality check. Maybe you aren't as good as you think you are."

Now I was intrigued. "Oh, really?"

"Yes. Really."

I loved a challenge, and it seemed like Zeke was bringing it. "I look forward to it."

Ray of Love

Chapter Two

Rex

Everyone met at Groovy Bowl when they got off work. It was the perfect place to have a meeting without that nosy little know-it-all snooping around. We sat at a high-top table in the bar area.

Kayden still wore her glasses because she came straight from work at the library. When she wore her contacts, she strained her eyes to read. Her eyes didn't get enough air and moisture with contacts, and they began to hurt after a while. Personally, I thought she looked cute in her black-framed glasses—very sexy.

Zeke wore his dark blue scrubs because he just got off work too. He didn't shave that morning, and I could see the facial hair coming in quickly. Jessie looked like a beauty queen, as always.

"Operation Rae's secret birthday party is in effect." I clapped my hands at the start of the meeting. "I was thinking we could get all get together at McHenry's. That's her favorite bar downtown. We could have some drinks, open some presents, and hit the dance floor."

"That's a pretty cool idea," Zeke said. "I know they have a private party room. Maybe we could rent that out so we'll have some space, just in case the bar is full. Besides, we could get a cake."

"Good thinking," I said. "I like cake."

"Who doesn't like cake?" Jessie said. "Chocolate is her favorite, so I'll take care of that. Since the Bulls are her favorite team, I'll have their logo put on top."

"Yeah, that's a great idea." I turned to Kayden. "Do you think you can get the decorations?"

"What decorations?" Kayden asked. "Is this a children's birthday party?"

I loved it when she was a smartass to me. Got me hard. "I thought we could have some balloons or something."

"At a bar?" Kayden asked incredulously. "No. No decorations. The cake and presents are enough. She's not five."

"With a Chicago Bulls cake, she seems five," I jabbed at no one in particular.

"We'll invite some of her friends from work and school," Zeke said. "So I think about twenty people will be there."

"That's a good number," Jessie said. "Not too many and not too few. I hope Ash will be there. Gawd, he's hot."

"Yeah, whatever," I said. "So I guess that's about it. Pretty easy to plan, actually."

"Rae is really simple," Kayden said. "The most easygoing person in the world."

I snorted because it was stupid. "Try living with her. I left a fork in the sink, and she screamed at me."

"Because it was covered with mustard," Zeke argued. "That shit stains."

"Whatever," I said. "The house has to be in tip-top shape. Otherwise, it's the end of the world."

"It is her place," Jessie said. "I mean, who wants to live like a pig?"

"And you did leave a dripping milk carton on the floor," Kayden said.

I turned my furious eyes on her, feeling betrayed when she took Rae's side over mine.

Kayden shrugged then looked away. "Just saying…"

"Looks like it's settled, then," Zeke said. "I think she's going to have a good time. She seemed a little down when I talked to her a few days ago. We should cheer her up."

"Oh yeah," Jessie said. "How did it go with Ryker?"

"Good," Zeke said. "Rae was totally fine with it. I can tell he wants her back."

"Say what?" I blurted. "What are you talking about?"

Zeke turned to me, that confident look in his eyes. "When he called her back over, I saw it in his expression. Then she touched him on the shoulder, and I saw it again too. He knows he was a dumbass and shouldn't have thrown her away. The only reason he hasn't tried to make it work is because he knows she's over him."

Jessie stared at Zeke like it was the first time she really looked at him. Surprise was in her eyes, as well as awe. "I didn't realize you were so observant."

When it came to Rae, he was always observant.

"Yeah," Kayden said. "You got all of that from a look?"

"Are you some kind of genius?" I asked. "You can read minds now?"

"No," Zeke replied. "But I've seen Ryker with her enough times to know what he's thinking. But it doesn't matter because she'll never take him back anyway, not after what he did."

"She better not," Jessie said. "Because I'd slap him every time I was in the same room as him."

"You wouldn't need to," I said. "Because I'd kill him the first time he set foot in the apartment." Ryker fucked my sister over once, and he would never get the opportunity to do it again.

Jessie looked around the bowling alley and saw how many people were coming and going. It was busy, especially for a Wednesday. "Business seems to be booming. There's got to be a few hundred people in here."

"Things have been great." I opened my wallet and pulled out a check. "Speaking of which...I finally have a payment for you." I set it on the table next to Zeke's beer. "That's the first half. I'll have the second in another month or so."

Zeke held it up and took a closer look at it. "Wow. I wasn't expecting this for a while."

"I've been frugal so I could pay you guys back quicker."

"You didn't need to do that," Zeke said. "I don't need this right away."

"But I want to be done with it," I said. "The sooner I get it out of the way, the sooner I can stop worrying about it. And I won't feel guilty about spending money on other things. Once my debt is paid, I can go buy a new PS4 and as many games as I want."

Zeke chuckled. "Well, I think Rae and I wouldn't have cared if you did."

"Whatever," I said. "Halfway finished."

"You're giving Rae a check too?" he asked.

"I will when I get home." She probably wouldn't even care about the money. All she wants is for me to move out as quickly as possible. I didn't like being there either, especially since Kayden and I were fooling around all the time. I had to sneak off and pretend I was doing other things besides screwing my sister's best friend. If I had my own place, it would be a lot simpler. "I'm halfway to moving the hell out of there."

Zeke folded the check and placed it in his wallet. "I can assure you, Rae is even more excited about that day than you are."

***

Rae was going to be home at any minute, and my job was to get her dressed up and ready to go out. Everyone would be waiting for her to show up at the bar, and they would jump out the second she walked inside.

Planning surprise birthday parties wasn't really my thing, but my sister had a tough year and I wanted to do something to lift her spirits. She hid her pain as much as possible once Ryker dumped her, but I knew she struggled the entire time. She deserved this—and not just because it was her birthday.

A knock sounded on the door.

Who the hell was that? They knew we were supposed to meet at the bar. I opened the door and expected to see a member of the gang. Instead, I came face-to-face with some random guy holding a vase of flowers. "Uh...what the hell is this?"

"Delivery for Rae." He handed them over and had me sign the clipboard. "Have a good day." He walked off to fulfill his next delivery.

I set the heavy vase on the table and looked at the two dozen freshly trimmed roses that reeked of springtime. I certainly didn't get her flowers, and I didn't know anyone who would. I spotted the card inside the envelope but knew I shouldn't read it.

None of my business.

Didn't matter.

Who cares?

But what if it was Ryker?

What if he was trying to fuck with her again?

I could just read the card and slip it back inside. Rae wouldn't know the difference.

Right?

Huge breach of privacy.

Definitely a dick move.

But I had the best intentions, so it was okay.

Wasn't it?

I stared at the card for another minute before I caved and opened the damn thing.

I pulled the card from the sleeve and read the words that had been typed.

Rae,

Thank you for coming last week. It meant a lot to me.

Have a special birthday.

-Ryker-

Fuck. Fuck. Fuck.

Zeke was right on the money. Ryker was totally trying to get back with her. Why the hell would he send her two dozen roses like this if his intentions weren't romantic? What a fucking douchebag. After the shit he put her through, he had the audacity to come crawling back?

Couldn't believe this.

I couldn't let her see this card. It would just ruin her birthday and confuse her. The past three months were difficult enough. She didn't need to be reminded of the man she confessed her undying love to, only to hear him not say it back.

I knew I shouldn't do what I was about to do, but I couldn't let her see any of this. It would just mess with her head.

I grabbed the vase and the card and went across the hall to the trash chute. I shoved everything inside and closed the hatch, hearing it shatter when it finally hit the bottom. The second I walked back inside, I washed my hands like I just disposed of a body. And not a moment too soon because Rae walked in immediately afterward.

"Hey." She set her purse on the counter and pulled her hair out of the bun she wore.

"Happy birthday." I hadn't seen her that morning because I went into work early.

"Thanks." She gave me a smile, something I hadn't seen much over the past three months. "I'm getting old."

"Since I'm four years older than you, remember when you get old, I get older."

"True," she said with a chuckle. "Well, I'm going to shower."

"Good. Because I want to take you out for a drink."

"You?" she asked suspiciously.

"Yes, me. And there's something I want to give you."

"First of all, I'm shocked that you even remembered my birthday. And now you got me a present too?"

"I know." I shrugged in modesty. "It's crazy."

"Give me thirty minutes, and I'll be ready to go."

"Great. And dress nice. I don't want people to think I'm hanging out with a hag."

She flipped me off before she walked away.

***

I sent a quick text to Zeke. *About to walk in. Get ready.*

K.

Rae noticed my fast fingers on the keyboard. "Anyone else coming?"

I shoved my phone into my pocket. "I just asked Zeke if he's doing anything tonight. Hasn't said anything yet."

"He texted me happy birthday earlier today. That was nice of him."

"I'm surprised he remembered."

"No. Zeke always remembers my birthday."

We walked into the bar, and I steered her toward the back room.

"Where are we going? The bar is this way."

Why was she such a pain in the ass? "I want to show you something."

"I already know where the bathrooms are."

Shut the hell up. "Jessie told me she's waiting in the back. Come on."

She finally dropped her resistance.

We walked to the back, and I opened the door so Rae could walk inside first.

Immediately, everyone jumped up and screamed, "Happy birthday!"

Rae nearly jumped out of her skin, covering her mouth as she screamed. "Oh my god! You guys scared the shit out of me."

"That's what birthdays are for, girl." Jessie held her drink up to the sky.

Rae looked over her shoulder at me. "You knew about this?"

"Obviously," I said like a smartass.

"Know about it?" Zeke said with a laugh. "He's the one who planned the whole thing."

Rae looked at me again, and this time, her expression was different. She didn't give me that hateful little sister expression I saw every single day. This look was full of affection and fondness. She didn't know what to say, and instead of smiling, her features softened. "That was sweet…"

I didn't like these emotional moments we sometimes had. They were rare, and they were rare for a reason. I'd never been the kind of guy to wear his heart on his sleeve or express how he felt about anything. Emotional intimacy terrified me, actually.

"Thank you, Rex." Rae walked up to me and extended her arms to hug me.

I returned the embrace, but I did it quickly, trying to get it over with so we could move on and have fun. "Of course. I do like you…sometimes."

"Only on my birthday?" When she smiled, she knew I was just teasing her.

"Only."

"Well, thank you for liking me for today." She walked away to say hi to everyone else. First, she greeted Zeke and gave him a hug.

He didn't hug her quickly and then move away. He wrapped his arms tight around her waist and held her against his chest. He even closed his eyes and whispered something in her ear.

Perhaps I was reading too much into it, but that hug didn't exactly seem platonic.

She moved away and greeted everyone else. Her presents were stacked on the table alongside the cake Jessie picked up for her. "Oh my god!" She covered her mouth as she stared at the cake designed with the logo of her favorite team. "This is the best cake ever."

"It was my idea!" Jessie raised her hand.

"Dude, it's perfect." Rae hugged her for a second time.

Zeke came to my side and gently nudged me. "This party was a success."

"It hasn't even started yet."

"But look how happy she is." Zeke watched her say hello to her friends, hugging everyone and enjoying being the center of attention. His gaze lingered longer than necessary before he looked back at me.

"Is Rochelle coming?"

"Yeah," he said with no visible reaction. "She had to work late, so she'll be here in an hour or so."

"Oh, cool."

Jessie climbed on one of the tables and held up her drink. "Let's get this party started!"

***

Kayden brushed up against me in the corner where it was dark and secluded. She wore a tight dress that made her tits look totally fuckable. Her hair was done, her makeup was sexy, and she wore heels that made her legs stretch on for days.

She knew exactly what she was doing.

I looked down at her with a warning in my eyes. "Baby, be good."

"No one is watching." Her hand moved to my crotch in the dark, and she traced the definition of my cock in my jeans. "And there's always the bathroom."

I closed my eyes and imagined her fingers wrapped tightly around my length. "I wish."

"Come on. Let's be adventurous."

"Or let's wait until the end of the night." I grabbed her wrist and pulled it away. "I'll stay over tonight."

"Promise?" She looked up at me and pouted her lips.

Now I wanted that soft mouth around my junk. "Promise."

Jessie walked right past us, and thankfully, she didn't notice anything concerning. "Let's open gifts!"

Rae was a little buzzed and staggered in her heels. "You guys got me presents? You guys..." She swayed slightly to the side.

"Of course." Jessie gripped her by the wrist, but since she was hammered, that didn't really help.

Zeke came to the rescue and guided Rae into a chair. "Here. Take a seat, and I'll pass the gifts along."

Rae held up her drink and clanked it against his arm like she was toasting him. "Zeke, you're the best. You know that?"

He chuckled and turned to the table where the gifts were waiting. "Yes. You've said that about ten times tonight."

"But you are!" Jessie said. "And so hot!"

Zeke smirked and pulled a chair up for her. "Alright. You need to sit down too."

Rae raised her glass. "So goddamn hot! Woo!"

Zeke immediately flinched when he heard Rae shout that for the entire world to hear. He watched her down her drink, his eyes focusing on her expression for nearly a minute. He finally shook it off and grabbed the first present he saw. "Here you go." He handed it over.

Rae dropped it on the ground. "Whoops..." She leaned into Jessie and giggled like her accident was particularly funny.

Kayden leaned toward me, her hand moving over my ass in my jeans. We were in the corner, so no one could see us from behind. "Everyone is so drunk no one would even notice if I gave you a hand job right now."

This woman was killing me. "Save it for when we get home, alright?"

"Why would I want to save anything when I can have you now?" She leaned dangerously close to me, almost placing a kiss on my lips.

I smacked her ass playfully. "Behave yourself."

She giggled into my ear. "How am I supposed to behave myself with your big hand on my ass?"

I couldn't believe this was the same Kayden who always had her nose in a book. She used to be shy and timid. Now, she was a behemoth of sexual desperation. "I'm gonna have to spank you when we get back to your place."

"Excellent."

Rae opened all of her gifts, getting an assortment of gift cards, clothes, and jewelry. She handed the extra bags and boxes to Jessie, who did a horrible job organizing everything because she didn't know her face from her ass.

"Alright." Zeke handed her a box. "This one is from me."

"Ooh…" Rae took it and held it to her chest. "Is it Operation?"

"No," Zeke said with a laugh. "And I'm not a surgeon."

"You're kinda like a surgeon when you pop pimples," Rae teased.

Zeke might normally be annoyed with a comment like that, but since Rae said it, it was perfectly okay. His only response was a smile. "Open it, and you'll see if you're right."

Rae ripped off the wrapping and tossed it at Jessie. She kept going until she got to the cardboard box underneath. She had to pull the flaps hard because of the tape, and she couldn't get through. "Someone have a pocket knife?"

Zeke snatched the box away from her and opened all the sides so she wouldn't stab herself in the eye like an idiot. He handed it back. "You should be good now."

She opened the lid of the box and looked down inside. "Sweet! A new basketball!" She pulled it out and felt it in her fingertips. "Mine was getting so worn out and dirty. This is perfect." She stood up and started to dribble.

"No!" Zeke grabbed the ball after it hit the ground once. "It's not to play with."

"Then what's it for?" Rae asked blankly.

Zeke turned the ball over and showed her something on the surface. Scribbled in black ink was some kind of writing, probably an autograph.

Rae squinted her eyes to make it out, but it took her a moment to piece it together. Then her eyes snapped open, and she gripped her chest like she might have a heart attack. "Oh my fucking god! Michael fucking Jordan?"

My jaw dropped.

She took the ball away from Zeke and stared at the writing with shaky hands. "Oh my god...oh my god...I can't breathe."

Zeke stared at her with the biggest grin I'd ever seen.

"How the hell did you get this?" she screamed.

Jessie leaned over. "Let me see. Let me see."

"That's so sick." Tobias peered over her shoulder. "That's really his signature. I recognize it." He read the message out loud. "To Rae, my biggest fan. Michael Jordan." Tobias gripped his skull and stepped back. "Greatest birthday gift ever." He bowed to Zeke. "You are the king, man."

Rae pulled the ball to her chest and looked at Zeke with tears in her eyes. "How on earth did you get this?"

"It's a long story. But basically, I went to a game with a few friends from work, and he was there. So I asked him to sign it." Zeke hadn't dropped his grin once since Rae opened her gift.

"Did you get one too?" she asked.

"Well...no." He shrugged. "But I know you're a much bigger fan than I am."

"I don't know what to say..." She handed the ball off to Jessie before she wrapped her arms around his neck and hugged him. "It's the best gift I've ever gotten, Zeke. Thank you so much." She rested her chin on his shoulder as she stood with her chest pressed against his.

Zeke held her by the waist, his face resting near hers. "You deserve it, Rae. You're my best friend."

They held each other for nearly a minute, Rae closing her eyes as she clung to his neck. Zeke stared at the floor as he kept his arms around her waist. Neither one of them said anything as the embrace continued.

"That was so thoughtful of Zeke," Kayden whispered.

"Yeah...really thoughtful." I knew I shouldn't be surprised, but I was. Zeke was happy with Rochelle but some of his feelings for Rae would never go away. He would look at her differently than the rest of us.

Forever.

***

Rae was hammered by the end of the night, and I knew it would be my responsibility to take her home. Because...you know...I lived with her.

"I'll take her," Zeke said. "I've got my truck, and I can put her stuff in the back."

"You sure?" I was looking for an excuse to take off with Kayden.

"Yeah."

"What about Rochelle?"

"Rochelle won't mind."

Rochelle was talking with Jessie and Kayden across the room, fitting in with the girls like she'd been around since the beginning. She said something funny, and the other two girls busted up laughing. She wasn't paying any attention to us.

"A Michael Jordan basketball?" I turned my eyes of accusation on Zeke. "Seriously?"

"What? I knew she would like that."

"You have to admit that gift is ridiculous. And I can only assume what that means..."

Zeke kept up his indifference. "I don't know what you're talking about."

"I thought you were over her? What about Rochelle?"

"I am over her," he snapped. "And I'm happy with Rochelle. She's amazing."

"Then what the fuck, Zeke? Why didn't you just get her a banner that said 'I love you' on it?"

He eyed the girls and made sure they weren't listening before he turned back to me. "I got that ball eight months ago. Obviously, when I got it, I was still in that place. It would be stupid for me not to give it to her now just out of principle. Shit, it has her name on it."

When he gave me that explanation, I realized I was overreacting. "Sorry for jumping down your throat."

"It's okay. I probably would have gotten her a gift card to Mega Shake or something if I didn't already have that."

"Yeah, you're right."

He clapped me on the shoulder. "Are you coming with us?"

I tried not to look at Kayden. "Nah. I'm gonna stay out for a while."

"Alright. I'll see you later." He went to Rae's side and pulled her to her feet. "Can you walk?"

"Bitch, I can run." She snapped her fingers then swayed on the stoop.

"That's a no..." Zeke scooped her into his arms, and the second he did, her head fell on his shoulder and she was asleep. "Damn, she's really wasted."

Rochelle grabbed a box of her things. "At least she had a good time."

Kayden grabbed a large bag containing the rest of her presents. "But she won't have a good time tomorrow..."

Rae mumbled against Zeke's chest. "Basketball..."

"Yes, Rae," Zeke said. "We got the basketball."

"I don't want to lose it," she whispered. "It's my favorite."

"I have it," Rochelle said. "Don't worry."

"Oh good," Rae whispered incoherently. "Rochelle will take care of it..."

Zeke laughed then carried her toward the door. "We'll get you home, and you can snuggle with that ball, alright?"

"Okay." She hooked her arms around his neck. "I'll sleep with that ball every night…"

Ray of Love

Chapter Three

Rae

"I think I'm gonna die…" I couldn't get out of bed. My head was pounding like a winter storm, and my insides were turned inside out from the level of alcohol they had to process and eliminate.

I hadn't felt this terrible in a long time.

"You aren't gonna die." Rex was dressed and ready to leave. He wore jeans and a sweater with his face cleanly shaven and his hair styled. "You're gonna be fine. Just take some aspirin and drink some water."

"Where's the aspirin?"

"I already threw you a birthday party. I've got to do that too?" Rex marched into the kitchen and grabbed the bottle before he returned. "Alright, I'm heading out. Don't call me."

All I could do was lie there with my big dog beside me, feeling and looking like shit. "Have fun…"

"I will."

"Are you gonna bring me back some food?"

"You know where the fridge is." He walked out of my room and down the hallway. I heard the front door open and then voices in a conversation.

"How is she?" Zeke's deep voice traveled down the hall and into my open bedroom.

"So fucking messed up," Rex said. "She looks like hell."

"Does she need anything?"

"She's fine," Rex said. "I'm on my way out."

"Where are you headed?"

Rex faltered before he answered. "I've got some errands, and then I'm supposed to meet up with an old friend at the bar."

"You aren't going to stay with Rae?"

"Hell no. I already threw her a surprise party. I've got to wipe her ass too?" Rex must have walked away because he didn't say anything else.

The door shut, and I assumed I was alone.

Zeke's heavy footsteps sounded in the hallway, and I knew he was coming my way. He rounded the corner and looked at me through the open doorway. "Hey." After a single look, he knew I was in terrible shape. "You look...tired."

"I look like hell. Rex was right."

"No, you don't."

"Oh, shut up." I rubbed my temple. "Yes, I do. Let's not sugarcoat it."

He watched me with his unreadable eyes, refusing to say I looked terrible because he was too nice. "Need anything?"

"No. Go enjoy the beautiful day." I grabbed the aspirin but couldn't get the top off. It had that stupid pressure mechanism so kids couldn't get into it. Since I felt like shit, I didn't have any patience for it.

"Let me." Zeke walked into the room and took the bottle of pills. He opened it without any problems then dumped out a few onto the nightstand. "How many?"

"Ten."

The corner of his mouth rose in a smile, and he placed two inside my palm. Then he handed me a bottle of water. "Two should be plenty."

"Alright, Dr. Zeke." I sat up and swallowed them with a gulp of water.

Zeke immediately pressed the back of his hand against my forehead to feel my temperature.

"Dr. Zeke is checking on me…"

He grabbed my wrist next and pinched a section of skin.

"Ouch. What's that for?"

"You're dehydrated. That's why you feel terrible and have a migraine."

I drank at least twenty cocktails last night. I was pumped with liquids. "Not possible. With the amount I drank last night, I'm plenty hydrated."

"You know better than that, Rae. Alcohol makes your body release more water in your urine. In turn, it makes you lose more water than you keep."

Actually, I did remember that from physio.

"So you need to drink lots and lots of fluids."

"Okay, Dr. Zeke…"

"Just Zeke." He pulled the blankets farther up my body then patted Safari on the head. "You need anything?"

"I'm okay. Go do something productive with your day."

"I don't mind staying if you need me. Rex clearly has plans."

"No…I'll be fine. I'll order a pizza or something." I tried to sit up, but I felt dizzy so I collapsed back on the bed. "Next time I drink that much…just stop me."

"You want me to be the drink police?"

"Please."

"You got it." He tapped my thigh. "I'm gonna put you on the couch then get you something to eat."

"You really don't have to do that…"

Zeke picked me up without further argument and carried me into the living room. He sat me on the couch, along with the comforter I'd been holding. He propped up a few pillows and made sure I was comfortable. "I'm going to Mega Shake. I'll be back in about twenty minutes."

"You don't need to do that."

"Is there something else you could possibly want?" Zeke knew me better than almost anyone, and anytime I had the choice of where I wanted to eat, it was always Mega Shake—every single time.

I looked away in response.

"That's what I thought."

***

Zeke returned with the burgers and fries and spotted me on the couch with my basketball. "If you wanted something to snuggle with, I could have gotten you a stuffed animal."

I squeezed the ball to my chest. "I would much rather snuggle with this rock-hard ball with Michael Jordan's signature than any girly stuffed animal. This is a relic." I turned the ball and stared at the signature, unable to believe my biggest icon had even touched this ball with his bare hands.

Zeke set the food on the coffee table then sat beside me. "What are you going to do with it?"

"What do you mean?"

"Put it in a case? Sleep with it every night?"

"I don't know. I love touching it, so I'm not sure I could put it inside a case."

"But you definitely aren't going to play with it, right?"

"God, no." This treasure wouldn't touch the dirty pavement. "I still can't believe you got this for me. It's...the most badass gift ever. When did this happen?"

"Remember when I was in Chicago for that convention?"

I jogged my memory and realized I did recall what he said about that game. "I remember you said you saw Michael Jordan in the stands."

"Yep. And he was sitting two seats away from me."

"That was like a year ago. I'm surprised you kept this ball from me for so long."

He bit into his burger and wiped the sauce away with the pad of his thumb, somehow making the activity of eating attractive. "I knew it would be a great birthday gift, so I decided to wait."

"And it was the best birthday gift. First, Rex throws me a party, and then you get me this..." I shook my head. "Man, I'm so lucky."

"I'm glad you feel that way." He put my food on a plate before he turned on the TV. A game was on, so he left the station on while he ate his food.

"Was Rochelle jealous?"

He stopped eating and forced himself to swallow even though he clearly wasn't ready to. "Jealous of what?"

"Jealous that you met Michael Jordan. She's a sports fan, right?"

"Oh." He downed his soda to clear his throat. "She prefers football. Her family are all big Seahawks fans, so she was kinda born into it."

"Okay, good. Because I'm really glad you gave the ball to me and not her."

"Well, that would be weird since your name is on it."

"Oh yeah..." I finally put it off to the side and dug into my meal. I made sure the ball was tucked away so I wouldn't accidentally swipe it with my greasy fingertips. Safari eyed the ball but knew better than to wipe his long tongue across it. "Do you have any plans tonight?"

"Rochelle wants to try this new Thai place that opened."

"Chop Stick?"

"Yeah."

"I went there with Jenny the other day. It's bomb."

"You say everything is bomb," he teased.

Ray of Love

"Look, I like food. And I like to describe the things I like appropriately."

"How would you describe it if you *loved* food?"

"Fucking bomb."

He drank more of his soda. "Then I guess it's not that good."

I stuck my hand into his tray of fries and stole a handful. "You know what? That's what you get."

"You're stealing my food? Who do you think brought it here?"

"Serious crimes need serious punishments."

Since I was concentrating on my fries, he snatched my burger and took an enormous bite out of it.

"How dare you!"

He spoke with his mouth full. "Don't do the crime if you can't do the time."

"Give it back to me."

He gave me an arrogant look before he took another enormous bite.

"You little bitch." I dove off the couch and collided with his chest. He fell back to the floor, and the burger went flying. Safari immediately chased after it in the hope he would get it first. "Oh, I don't think so." I reached right to grab it, but Zeke pulled me away.

"Nope," he said. "That's what you get."

Safari ate the burger in a single bite then licked his lips.

My lunch was gone, and now all I had were fries. "No!"

"Too bad, so sad." Zeke sat up and moved me effortlessly. The muscles of his core contracted, and he felt like a wall of steel. He set me on the ground beside him.

I was still in shock. "What am I supposed to eat?"

"You should have thought about that before you messed with me."

My stomach growled, so I pouted my lips in his direction.

Zeke sighed before he grabbed his burger and tore it in half. He handed me one piece then took a bite of the other.

I grabbed it with both hands so no one could steal it from me this time. "Thanks."

"You're lucky I'm so nice." He leaned against the couch as he ate, digging his hands into the fries in between bites.

"I know." After he gave me that basketball, I shouldn't have tackled him at all, no matter how much he teased me. "But I think you're fucking bomb."

He stopped himself from taking another bite and smiled. "Is that your way of telling me you love me?"

I stared into his eyes and saw one of the most important people in the world. Rex was my family by blood, but Zeke was just as good even though we didn't share a strand of DNA. He was someone who had always been in my life, and he would always be there. He was special, more than words could say. "Yes."

***

"What are the teams?" Zeke dribbled beside me as we walked down the sidewalk to the courts.

"Tobias and me against you two." Rex and Tobias walked in front of us, talking about their night out at the bars.

"You never want to be on my team," I argued. "Even though you always get your ass kicked."

"I'd rather get my ass kicked than be your ally." Rex didn't turn around as he spoke, nearly giving me the cold shoulder.

"But it's not even competitive." I wore my leggings and a gray sweater. Once we started playing, I would get hot and have to remove it, but for now, it was too cold outside. "Zeke and I are too good."

"Fine," Rex said. "I'll be on Zeke's team. You and Tobias pair up."

I wanted Rex to be on my team for once. When he covered me, he was particularly vicious. He had no problem throwing elbows around and pushing me off to the side like a rag doll. The other guys wouldn't even touch me. Ironically, if Zeke or Tobias even bumped me by accident, Rex would turn into a nightmare. "Whatever."

We got to the court and started the game. Tobias was a good player, but we didn't have the same chemistry Zeke and I did. Somehow, we could communicate without actually saying anything. Zeke knew exactly when to get open and when to fake his passes. And I always figured out what he was doing.

Tobias and I were in the lead, but not by much. Switching up the teams definitely made things more competitive, but that was because Zeke and Rex were practically one person. I thought Zeke and I clicked, but they were connected on a whole new level.

At halftime, I was drenched in sweat and my body ached. I ripped off my sweater and tossed it on the ground outside of the court, not even caring I was getting my nice Nike sweater dirty. My hairline was wet from perspiring, and I could hardly catch my breath.

"We're still in the lead." Tobias rested his hands on his hips as he caught his breath. We stood under our hoop and tried to take a short break before we were back at it. "If we keep it up, we'll still win."

"Yeah...but it's only halftime." I wiped my forearm across my forehead to remove the sweat. But of course, my head produced more a second later.

"We'll be fine. We make a good team."

"Yeah." I looked across the court and saw our opponents talking. Rex grabbed his water bottle and took a long drink. Zeke pulled off his long-sleeve shirt and stood shirtless underneath the hoop. His fair skin was flawless with muscles etched everywhere. His shoulders were rounded and outlined with strength. I could see every little muscle connect down his arm, forming a perfect physique that could be used in an anatomy lab. He had no fat, so every detail was noticeable.

His chest was wide and powerful, his two pecs were slabs of muscle that could move a mountain. His stomach was the best. An eight-pack that had little rivers running everywhere. His slender waist narrowed into his hips where a small patch of his happy trail could be seen.

Day-yum.

I'd seen him shirtless before, but it was so long ago, I couldn't remember. And I already knew he had a nice body. Even in t-shirts, his arms and shoulders looked great. But now that I was face-to-face with his pure physical beauty, I couldn't stop staring.

Shit, he was hot.

Had he always been that sexy?

I seriously needed to stop staring. Zeke was my friend, and it was weird.

Just stop staring.

God, I couldn't stop.

I had the random urge to catcall him, something I'd never wanted to do in my life.

"You all right?" Tobias' voice penetrated through my haze.

"All right?" I asked. "Shit, I'm great. I'm superb. I'm totally cool. Why wouldn't I be?" I sounded defensive, even to my ears.

"Well...I've been trying to get your attention for nearly a minute."

"Sorry, I was thinking about a play we could do."

"Cool. What play?"

"Uh...never mind. I don't think it'll work. Rex already knows it."

"Damn."

We met in the center of the court and began the second half of the game. Now that I was five feet away from Zeke, I had chills. My spine couldn't relax, and there was a numbness inside my fingers.

Don't stare.

Don't.

Goddammit, I looked!

Get a hold of yourself, Rae.

It was just because I hadn't gotten laid in three months. That was all. My hormones were out of whack, and my body was eager for this dry spell to end. That was it. Nothing more.

Once we started the second half, I focused on the game and not Zeke's ridiculously perfect physique. I paid attention to Tobias and getting that ball through the hoop and scoring as many points as possible.

Until Zeke covered me.

With his massive chest, he blocked my view of the hoop. His hand was in my way, so I couldn't toss the ball to Tobias as he ran by.

Shit, this was distracting.

Sweat formed on Zeke's chest and trickled down the delicious muscles of his body. I wanted to touch him just to see how hard he was. And I wanted to touch him somewhere else to see how hard he could get.

Oh wow.

This was bad.

Really bad.

Zeke slapped the ball out of my hand and sprinted to the other side of the court, getting a turn over and scoring a point against me.

No one had ever stolen the ball from me before.

I wasn't thinking.

Rex jogged by. "Losing your touch, loser?"

I didn't know what was happening, but losing my touch was the least of my problems.

***

His face was between my legs, and his mouth did exquisite things to my throbbing pussy. His tongue gently moved inside me, making sweet love to me with just his mouth. Then he pulled out and circled my clit, pushing me to the edge of an orgasm.

God, it felt good.

My fingers dug into his hair and nearly pierced his scalp. I moaned as I moved my hips and pressed my pussy farther into his face.

He moved his large hands to my thighs and separated them wide, exposing more of me to enjoy. "I could do this all day."

"Then please do." I gripped his arms and dug my nails into his skin.

He sucked me hard into his mouth before he crawled up my body. "But I want to fuck you even more." He pressed my thighs back and shoved himself deep inside me with one simple thrust.

"Oh god…" I gripped his biceps and felt him thrust into me with his enormous package. "Zeke."

"I love this pussy. And I love you."

"Yes…I love you too."

He pounded into me hard, fucking me like an animal but somehow making it feel romantic.

And then I came. "Zeke…Zeke."

He kissed me on the mouth until my high died away.

The sensation brought me into consciousness just as the orgasm faded away. I opened my eyes and realized I was in my bedroom, but Zeke wasn't there. The area between my legs was wet, but not from his saliva.

The details of the dream didn't leave my mind, even when I woke up. It seemed like it had just happened—his hands were all over me and his cock was pressed deep inside me. The haze over my eyes made me want to return to that dream, to feel that intimacy.

But I couldn't believe I had a sex dream about Zeke.

That was new.

Ray of Love

Chapter Four

Rex

My alarm went off, and I hit the snooze button three times before I finally got up. "I hate working..."

Kayden threw the covers off and got out of bed. She wore one of my t-shirts, looking sexy as hell in the baggy clothes. "It's not that bad. Just getting up is the hard part."

"I can't wait until I make enough money to hire a manager. Then I can just pop in once in a while."

"I think you'd get bored." She came to my side of the bed then straddled my hips.

I leaned against the headboard and felt her sit on me. When I felt her bare skin, I realized she wasn't wearing any panties. She did the sluttiest things sometimes, and damn, they were sexy.

I pulled down my boxers so my cock popped up, and I was ready to go. I slid inside of her, not surprised she was already wet. I gently sank into her and closed my eyes for a moment, enjoying her.

She slowly rode me, her eyes locked to mine. "What would you do all day if you didn't work?"

"Fuck you."

She continued to grind against me. "Well, I have to work, so I won't be here."

"Quit your job. I'll pay you to do this all day."

"While that sounds tempting, I'm not sure if that's a respectable career."

"Oh, it is." I grabbed her hips and pulled her farther down my length. I loved every inch of her pussy. I'd never fucked the same woman for so long, and I'd been doing this for four months now. But it never got old.

She increased her pace slightly, taking my length more and more. Soon, she started to pant, making those sexy little noises I'd come to love.

I was right at the edge and ready to dump everything inside her. But I held on and waited for her to finish. Having a beautiful woman ride my cock first thing in the morning like she needed it to get out of bed was sexy as hell.

Within seconds, she reached her climax, moaning with satisfaction. She threw her head back and rode my cock all the way down from her high, her nails digging into my bare shoulders. Her breathing became deep and shallow as the sensation passed.

After she was finished, I could come without feeling like a jackass. I pressed my length completely inside her before I released, wanting to ensure her beautiful pussy got every drop I possessed.

The climax was amazing, the perfect way to start my day. "Now I want to go to work even less."

"Just remember, when you get off work, I'll be waiting. Actually, we'll both be waiting..."

***

Zeke and I met at our favorite wing place for dinner. We ordered the atomic wings with fries and two enormous beers. The game was on in the corner, but I had a hard time concentrating because I was thinking about that little vixen.

"Can I ask you something?"

Zeke finished his wing then wiped his fingers on a napkin. "What's up?"

"So...I've been sleeping with this girl for a while."

"What's a while?" he asked.

"A few months..."

Zeke's eyes popped open like they might roll out of his head. "A few months? You?"

"I know...pretty weird, huh?"

"Super weird," he said. "That's a record for you."

"Yep." A big one.

"The longest relationship I remember you having was three weeks with Vanessa."

"Oh yeah...I forgot about her." I had been walking down the street when she stepped out of a tattoo parlor. She'd just gotten her tongue pierced, so we decided to give it a try. And spoiler alert, getting head with a piercing was awesome.

"Three months... That's a relationship."

"Whoa, back up." I placed my hand in front of his face. "I know it's not a relationship. She said she wanted a fling, and I wanted a fling."

"Flings don't last months."

"But the sex is so good, man." Just thinking about it got me hard. "She's perfect."

"Have you slept with anyone else in this timeframe?"

"Why would I?" I blurted. "When I can just text her and ask for awesome sex?"

He gave me a knowing look, like he was aware of something I wasn't. "Rex, this actually sounds kinda serious. Who is this girl?"

I definitely couldn't tell him that. "Just some woman."

"Does this woman have a name?"

I tried to think of something on the spot. "Bonnie." I'd never even met a Bonnie and neither had he.

"You've been sleeping with Bonnie for a few months," he said. "You must feel something more than just lust."

"I don't." We fucked and had a great time. That was it.

"Well, I can promise you she definitely feels something."

"Trust me, man. She doesn't." I knew Kayden in a way he never would.

"I know women. And women won't be a fling for that long. They'll move on to find someone who will commit."

"Not this chick."

"Even if she doesn't feel something now, which she does, it's only a matter of time before that happens. If you really don't feel anything for this girl and never will, you need to cut her loose. Because you're going to rip her heart out."

Those words hit me hard. The idea of hurting Kayden made me sick to my stomach. I wanted to keep up our arrangement, but I'd rather die than break her heart. She wasn't just my friend. She was like family. If some other guy hurt her, I'd break down his door and murder him in cold blood.

Zeke watched me as he drank his beer. "You understand what I'm saying?"

I nodded because I knew he was right.

"I would do it soon. Get out before it gets messy, you know?"

"Yeah..." I released a sigh of despair.

Zeke caught on to it. "But if you really like her, just do the relationship thing."

"That's not for me, man. You know it."

"That's not true. If you meet someone you really like, you can do anything."

"But I've never been the monogamous type. I don't see myself getting married. I can't even figure out what I'm doing next week."

"You don't need to know what you're doing next week, or even forever. You just need to know who you want by your side when you do figure it out."

It was the wisest thing I've ever heard him say, and I was speechless.

"Speaking of forever..." He pushed his beer aside and dug into his pocket. "Rochelle and I have been happy for a long time now..."

As in, six months. But whatever.

"And I think she'll be a great partner to share my life with. She'll be a great mom, a great wife..." He pulled out a small box and placed it on the table. "So I'm going to ask her to marry me."

Holy fucking shit.

This was real.

Fuck. Fuck. Fuck.

Zeke waited for me to react, to wear a big smile and congratulate him.

But I didn't know how to do that. I was in shock. This relationship had moved way too fast from the beginning, and it still didn't feel right.

"Rex?" His smile faded when he saw my speechless look.

"I just... I guess I'm surprised."

"Why?"

"It seems a little soon, don't you think?" I knew I was an ass for saying that, but I had to be the voice of reason. Fucking around and playing house was fine, but marriage was some serious shit.

"Soon?" Zeke said the word like he wasn't even sure what it meant.

"Zeke, you've only been with Rochelle for six months..."

"Yeah, but it feels right."

It felt right because he wanted to hurry up and settle down so he wouldn't be hurt over Rae anymore.

But could I really say something that harsh to him? "Zeke, I really like Rochelle. She's a very nice girl—"

"But what?"

"I think...sometimes...you might be..."

"Just spit it out, Rex."

I hated myself for saying this. But I would hate myself more if I didn't. "She's a rebound, man."

"A rebound?" He stared me down coldly, like the insinuation was unforgivable. "From who? I wasn't dating anyone before Rochelle."

"Don't make me say it, man..."

Zeke kept his gaze locked on to mine.

"You were going to go for Rae, but then Ryker got in the way. Right after that, you found Rochelle. I think you were more devastated than you let on, and now you want to hurry up and get married because you don't know what else to do."

He crossed his arms over his chest and clenched his jaw.

"I hate saying that. I really do. But that's what I think."

"I love Rochelle, Rex. In case you haven't noticed, she makes me happy."

"And I'm glad she does. This has nothing to do with her personally."

"Is it really so unlikely that I happened to find the woman I'm supposed to be with?"

"Because you convinced yourself of that?" People did crazy things to protect themselves from pain.

"I'm over Rae, Rex. I've been over her for a long time. She's single now, and you don't see me going for her. Because I love Rochelle."

"No. It's because you know she doesn't feel the same way." I hated doing this, but could I call myself his best friend if I wasn't straight with him? If I didn't talk to him before he made the biggest mistake of his life?

He clenched his jaw tighter.

"This relationship is going way too fast. If you'd been dating her for at least a year, it would be different. But you guys powered through this relationship toward the end and skipped the beginning and the middle. Don't act like that's not true."

"Every relationship is different, Rex."

"Why do you need to marry her right now?" I countered. "Why don't you wait a few more months? Preferably a year?"

"Why wait? I'm ready to get married and start a family."

"But you need to wait for the right person. Are you sure it's Rochelle?"

"She's perfect," he countered. "Tell me one bad thing about her."

Like I would be stupid enough to do that. "Dude, there's nothing wrong with Rochelle. I never said there was. But I still think you're doing this for the wrong reasons."

He took the ring back. "Whatever." He shoved the box into his pocket then left the table.

I let him go because I knew we both needed some distance. What I said was hurtful, and I couldn't blame him for being upset with me. After he took some time to think about it, he would see that I was right.

***

A week went by, and I didn't hear from him.

I was supposed to call it off with Kayden, but I was too depressed to end things with her while I was stressed about my best friend. So I kept having sex with her around the clock, and fortunately, it made me feel a little better.

By the end of the second week, I couldn't take the silence anymore.

I wanted us to be friends again. I even wanted to apologize for hurting him.

I went to his house and knocked on the door.

He answered it with a grim look, not seeming happy to see me at all. But if he really didn't want to talk to me, he wouldn't have answered the door. Wordlessly, he walked away.

That was the only invitation I was going to get.

I followed him into the house and to the couch in the living room. The game was on, but the TV was on mute.

He sat on one couch.

I sat on the other.

He didn't look at me, which told me he wanted me to speak first.

"I want to apologize for last week. I hope you understand I would never hurt you on purpose. As your best friend, it's my job to tell you things you don't want to hear. I meant well—really."

He rubbed his palms together and stared at the floor, his jaw clenched like before. "Yeah...I know."

At least he was reasonable about it.

"If you want to marry Rochelle, you know you have my full support. I'll be your best man, and I'll be damn happy for you. But I needed to say that just in case you realized this wasn't right for you."

He continued to move his palms together slowly.

I didn't say anything else, giving him the floor. Judging by the tightness in his jaw, he did have something he wanted to say.

"I admit, when Rochelle and I got together, I was going through a hard time. It wasn't the fact that I couldn't be with Rae that bothered me. It was the fact that I didn't step up when I had the chance. Ryker swept her off her feet, made her fall in love, and then broke her. I missed my chance out of pure stupidity. When I met Rochelle, I knew she was really into me. She was sweet, pretty, and kind. I threw myself into the relationship to feel better. Now, when I look back on it, I know you're right."

At least he admitted it.

"But our relationship is different now. We've grown from what we were when we first started dating. I have no doubt in my mind she'll make me happy for the rest of my life. She's smart, accomplished, and incredible. I really couldn't ask for someone better."

I still didn't think they should get married so soon, but it was obvious Zeke had made up his mind. I said what I needed to say, and that was all I could do. "Then I'm happy for you. When are you going to ask?"

"In a few weeks. My friend has a yacht in the harbor, so he said I could use it for a romantic dinner. Then I'll get down on one knee and ask for her hand."

"Wow. That's damn romantic."

He finally smiled for the first time. "It is."

"The girls will be excited."

"About that...don't tell them."

"What? Why not?"

"You know how they are. They couldn't keep a secret if their lives depended on it. The second they're around Rochelle, they'll act different and give it away."

"Yeah…true."

"Keep it to yourself."

"You got it."

Now that the hard conversation was over, he leaned back into the couch and put his feet on the coffee table. "Break up with Bonnie?"

"Who?"

"That girl you've been seeing."

"Oh…no. I haven't gotten around to it." I was too stressed about Zeke to even consider it. All the sex she gave me made me feel better. Without it, this week would have been much worse.

"Let me know how it goes. Hopefully, it's not too late."

"Too late for what?"

"Hopefully, she hasn't already fallen in love with you."

***

"Hey." I walked in the door and saw her sitting on the couch.

"Hey." Kayden immediately jumped up with a smile on her face, so excited to see me. Like Safari waiting for Rae, she looked like she'd been waiting for me to come home all day. She wrapped her arms around me and kissed me hard on the mouth.

I loved that mouth. So warm and soft. She had the plumpest lips, the kind I could devour all day long. The thought of no longer kissing those lips anymore made me sadder than I expected, but I knew it was the right thing to do. This had gone on for too long, and if I didn't end it soon, it would just ruin our friendship.

"I missed you."

"I missed you too." I kissed her a little longer before I finally pulled away.

"What were you doing?"

"I went by Zeke's place. We kinda had an argument, and I wanted to work things out."

"About what?"

I'd keep his secrets. "Just stupid guy stuff. We made a bet, and I never paid him when I lost..."

"Well, I'm glad you guys worked it out. So, what do you want to do? Go straight to the bedroom?"

If we did that, we would never talk. "Actually, I wanted to talk about something..."

She knew it was serious by my tone. Her arms left my waist, and she took a step back, the joy in her eyes completely gone. "Oh?"

"About us... I've been having a lot of fun. The sex is incredible, you're incredible, everything is incredible. But..."

"But, what?"

"I think we should put an end to it. We've been fooling around for a few months now, and I'm afraid it will affect our friendship if we keep going. Soon, it might become more serious than either of us wants, you know?"

She stared at me blankly, her face a concrete wall. She didn't even blink.

What was she thinking? "I don't want the group dynamic to be off. People might notice something if we can't be around each other anymore. I just don't want to ruin what we have. Too much of a good thing can lead to a bad thing."

Still, nothing. She crossed her arms over her chest and stepped back.

Was she pissed at me? "Kayden?"

She cleared her throat then ran her hand through her hair, snapping out of it. "Sorry, I was thinking about something else..."

Right now?

She cleared her throat again. "Yeah, you're probably right. Maybe we should stop...for the sake of our friendship."

I knew she would be cool about this. There was no possibility she'd fallen for me. If she did, she would have said something by now. We were just two friends using each other to get off. People did that sort of thing all the time. "You wanna go for one more round? You know, seal the deal?" Anytime I was alone with her, my cock was hard and eager to get down to business. Maybe one more fuck would get her out of my system.

"Actually...I have to be somewhere. I forgot I have plans with a friend from the library. We're getting rid of the card catalog system and replacing everything with computers, so we're going to get a drink and discuss how we're going to do that."

On a Friday night?

"I should get in the shower. But I'll see you around." She walked away without even letting me out. Her feet echoed down the hallway, and she closed the bathroom door behind her. A moment later, the water started to run.

Her hair and makeup were already done so it didn't seem like she needed a shower. But I didn't understand women, so perhaps I was missing something. I turned to the door and let myself out.

Chapter Five

Rae

"Kayden's not coming?"

Jessie walked with me inside the bar, our arms linked together. She looked like a beauty queen, as always. "She said she had plans tonight but didn't say what. That's all I know."

"Well, we do have friends outside the five of us. Can't blame her for wanting to take a break once in a while."

Jessie stopped walking in the midst of the crowd. "Zeke and Rochelle are over there."

I saw them standing close together, both wearing stupid smiles on their faces from being so damn happy.

God, I felt guilty for that dream I had.

And the other two after that.

"But..." Jessie nodded in the opposite direction. "There's a really fine hunk over there."

"It's okay. You talk him up, and I'll say hi to Zeke and Rochelle. You want me to get you a drink?"

She slipped out of my hold with a mischievous look on her face. "If things go according to plan, he'll be buying me one."

"True." I watched her walk to the tall stranger in the corner before I joined Zeke and Rochelle. "Hey, what's up?"

"Hey, Rae." Rochelle hugged me like she usually did.

I purposely stayed far away from Zeke and hardly said hello to him. I couldn't bring myself to look him in the eye, not after all the dirty dreams I'd had. He gave it to me good, and every time I was sleeping, he made me come—hard. If Rochelle knew what I was thinking... Well, she had my full permission to scratch my eyes out.

Zeke immediately noticed my peculiar behavior. "All right?"

"Just a little buzzed," I lied.

Zeke didn't press me on it, probably because Rochelle was there. He glanced toward the door and saw someone he recognized. "Baby, the guys are here. I'm excited for you to meet them."

I saw three guys walk in. Judging by their ages and looks, they had to be friends from school because I didn't recognize them.

Zeke walked us over, and he made his introductions. "Guys, this is Rochelle." They all shook hands with her before they shook hands with me. "We went to undergrad together. Thought we'd all hang out tonight."

The guys were quiet, staring at Rochelle like they knew her but couldn't place her.

"She works in pediatrics," Zeke explained like that would answer their unspoken questions.

Zeke's phone began to ring, so he checked the screen. "Goddammit, it's Rex. He's probably lost somewhere…" He pushed through the crowd and headed toward the entrance.

Rochelle seemed uncomfortable by their stares, so she excused herself to the bathroom. "I have to pee. I'll be right back. You mind holding this?" She extended her drink to me.

"Yeah, of course." I took it, and like an alcoholic, I held two glasses.

She walked away, and I was left with these guys I'd never met.

I tried to make conversation. "So you guys went to Washington State too?"

Like they didn't hear me, they talked about something else. "Didn't realize Zeke was so into Lane Bryant." He chuckled as he said it, and his two friends laughed along.

What?

Another one said, "But I guess it's more cushion for the pushin'."

They busted up laughing like it was the most hilarious thing in the world.

"She's definitely not a cheap date." The man in the center laughed at his own joke, again. "Not if he takes her to a restaurant."

It took me a second to realize what really was going on. At first, I thought I misunderstood what they were saying. After all, I was Zeke's friend, and they were saying that shit right in front of me. "Excuse me?"

They kept chuckling until their laughter died down.

"Who the fuck do you think you are?" My rage came out of nowhere. I didn't even know I had it in me to explode like a volcano. "And you think you're perfect, Mr. Big Nose and Mr. Chest Hair?" I threw both of my glasses into their faces and splattered the liquid across their clothes. "Grow up, dickfaces. You should be ashamed of yourselves. I know I am."

I walked around them, about to storm off to tell Zeke exactly what his so-called friends said behind his back. But I ran into Rochelle instead.

And tears were pouring out of her eyes.

Oh no.

She covered her face and dashed away, moving past the crowd and making it through the back door. She walked outside and was greeted by the cold air, her hair flying about in the breeze.

I went after her and joined her on the sidewalk. Fortunately, no one was back there, so she had some privacy. One car drove by, but that was our only company. "Rochelle…" I saw her body shake as the tears continued to rock her body. "Don't listen to those assholes. They don't know what they're talking about."

"But they're right." She held her tears back long enough to say a few words. "Zeke is out of my league. He's perfect, gorgeous, and his body…is beautiful. I'm just some fat girl."

"Rochelle, don't say that. That's not true at all."

"Yes, it is." She continued to cover her eyes so I couldn't see her cry.

"Don't let them kick you down like this. Their actions say a lot more about them than they do about you. You're beautiful and perfect just the way you are. You really believe Zeke thinks any different? He loves you for you. So who gives a shit what some insecure assholes say? Their opinions are irrelevant."

She wiped her face, smearing her makeup in the process, and then sat on the curb of the sidewalk. She pulled her knees to her chest and sniffed a few times, her tears finally subsiding.

I sat beside her and was relieved she finally calmed down. Seeing her cry was heartbreaking, and I had to stop myself from marching back into that club and doing something worse than throwing drinks in their faces. "From the beginning, all of us have loved you for Zeke. Hands down, you're our favorite."

"Really?" she whispered.

"Absolutely. You make Zeke so happy. And I can tell you love him. You're perfect for him."

"That's nice of you to say..."

"I told those guys off and threw drinks in their faces, just so you know. And I'm sure Zeke will kick their asses once he finds out."

"I wish I could have seen that..."

"I'm sure someone recorded it on their phone. Maybe we can track it down on YouTube."

She chuckled slightly. "Yeah, maybe."

I rubbed her back gently. "It'll be alright, Rochelle. There will be people in our lives that hurt us. But we have to laugh it off and keep going."

"I know, I know. Sometimes it's hard."

"Yeah...I know."

When she looked at me, her eyes were red and swollen. They were puffy from the way her fingers touched her skin, and her cheeks were still blotchy from sobbing. But her eyes still had their natural blue beauty. "When I first met you, I was so intimidated by you."

"Me?" I pointed a finger into my chest because her sentence was ridiculous. "The nerdy tomboy?"

"When Zeke told me how he used to feel about you...I felt threatened. And then when I met you and realized how pretty you are, I was even more insecure. But you've always been so nice to me. And you're such a good person. Now I don't blame Zeke for feeling the way he did. If I were a guy, I'd probably feel the same way."

I heard what she said, but it took me nearly a minute to process it. "Feeling what way?"

"How he used to be in love with you." She moved her fingertips around her eyes, doing her best to fix her makeup. Her mascara had run to her cheeks, and her eyeliner was smeared around her eyelids.

The nighttime air was cold, but now it was freezing. My hand stopped in the center of her back and felt her distant beating heart. Time seemed to slow down as her meaning hit me right in the chest.

Zeke used to have feelings for me?

I just...couldn't believe that.

When?

How?

He used to be in love with me?

Rochelle watched my reaction, and slowly, her eyes narrowed. "Did you...not know that?"

I opened my mouth to speak, but I couldn't bring myself to say anything. "I...no."

"Oh..." Her eyes reddened in embarrassment then she covered her face again. "I'm so sorry. I thought you knew. He made it sound like everyone knew about it."

"It's okay..." What else was I supposed to say? I was in total shock.

"Anyway...you're a really good person, Rae. Not very many people would have had my back in there."

Her words brought me back to the conversation and the whole reason why we were sitting on the sidewalk to begin with. I could process what she said later. But right now, I couldn't dwell on it. "Of course, Rochelle. You're my friend. Anyone else in the gang would have done the same thing. Well, except Rex. Rex would have knocked them all out right then and there."

"Zeke has the greatest friends…"

I pulled my hand away from her back and rested it on my lap. I stared at the reflection of the streetlights on the damp road. The stars couldn't be seen because it was overcast. But for Seattle, it was still a beautiful night.

"Rae?"

"Hmm?"

"Could you not tell Zeke about what happened in there? I don't want him to get upset and do something he'll regret. And…it's really embarrassing."

If that's what she wanted, I would give it to her. "Of course. But could you do something for me?"

"Yeah. What?"

"Could you not tell Zeke you told me that?" I didn't know what I was going to do with the information, but I certainly didn't want him to know that I knew. It might make things awkward between us. After all the sex dreams I'd been having about him, I already felt awkward.

"Sure."

"Thanks." I stared down at my hands and suddenly felt uncomfortable sitting next to her. Just the night before, I'd dreamed that Zeke took me from behind and rocked my world. Then he whispered he loved me in my ear. I was a terrible person for having those dreams, even if they were out of my control. If she had those dreams about Ryker when I was seeing him, I'd go ape-shit crazy on her ass.

***

I walked in the door after midnight. "Rex!" I threw my purse down and immediately stormed into the living room.

Rex and Tobias were sitting on the couch playing a car racing game. Both of their backs were to me, and neither one looked over their shoulder. "What's your deal?" Rex hit the buttons on the controller, making it tap loudly. "Forgot your bitchy pills today?"

"Tobias, please leave. I need to talk to Rex alone."

"Ignore her," Rex said. "She's just being annoying."

I grabbed the remote and turned off the TV. "I'm trying not to be rude, Tobias. But please leave. I have something very important to discuss with Rex."

Tobias left without a word, knowing I meant business.

Rex stood to his full height, his expression morphing into one of rage. "What the hell—"

"Zeke used to have feelings for me?"

His mouth was still gaping open, and slowly, he started to close it. The anger that was in his eyes a second ago disappeared quicker than the snap of a finger. His eyes shifted back and forth as he tried to plan his next move. "What are you talking about?"

"You know exactly what I'm talking about." I crossed my arms over my chest and stared my brother down with determination.

"Where would you get that idea? Zeke has feelings for you as a friend, obviously. But that's it."

"Well, Rochelle told me otherwise."

His mouth opened again, and he lost his poker face. "She told you?"

"She told me Zeke used to have feelings for me before they met. And you're going to explain that to me."

"Explain what?"

"How long did this go on? Why didn't anyone tell me? Why didn't he confront me about it? How did everyone know except me?" I felt like a fool when something that big was going on right under my nose. "Did you know about this?"

"Uh…"

"Rex."

He ran his fingers through his hair, clearly unsure what he should do. He was Zeke's best friend, so he obviously knew all the details. But he didn't want to betray Zeke's trust.

"I already know the truth, so just give me the specifics."

"Alright." He dropped his hands to his sides. "Yeah...it's true."

Now that Rex confirmed it, it felt all the more real. The man who I thought was my best friend wanted something more that entire time. Now I reevaluated every hug and every touch. I wondered what he was really thinking when he looked at me. "When?"

"For the past three years."

"What?" I covered my mouth as I gasped, unable to believe this lasted much longer than I ever could have guessed. "Are you serious?" I dropped my hands back to my hips. "Three years?"

"He said it was on and off. He'd start seeing someone and wouldn't think about you anymore. But the second he was single, he would think about you again. I don't want to make it sound like it was three years nonstop because it wasn't."

"But...that's still a long time."

He shrugged like he didn't know what to say.

"And you knew that whole time?"

"No. He told me a few months ago."

"Why did he tell you?"

Rex took a deep breath before he answered. "He was going to tell you how he felt, but he wanted my blessing first."

"But he never told me. What happened?"

He lowered his eyes like he didn't want to answer. "Ryker."

My lungs forgot to breathe whenever he was mentioned. "Oh..."

"The night you and Zeke went out to dinner…he was going to tell you then. But you told him you were seeing Ryker, so he didn't say anything."

"Oh my god…"

"And then he moped around for a little while before he started seeing Rochelle. That's about it."

I paced around the apartment because I couldn't stand still. "I just can't believe this. I can't believe I never noticed."

"In your defense, I didn't notice either."

"But I can't believe the girls didn't tell me. I understand why you didn't say anything because he's your best friend…but what about Jess? Kayden?"

"They didn't know. I was the only one who did."

"Oh." At least that made more sense.

"Yeah…so the cat's outta the bag."

I sat on the couch because my legs couldn't carry me anymore.

"I'm surprised Rochelle mentioned it to you."

"She thought I already knew."

"But why bring that up at all?"

I didn't want to tell him the story because I knew it would embarrass her. And he might bring it up to Zeke. "We were talking, and she said she used to be intimidated by me...then she explained why."

"That was still an awkward thing to say."

I slipped off my heels and leaned against the couch. "I guess."

Rex took the seat beside me. "Now, what? Are you going to confront him about it?"

"No. Why would I?"

He shrugged. "I don't know...you seemed bothered by the news."

"I'm not bothered...just surprised."

"After he told me the truth, I realized it wasn't that crazy. The two of you have a lot in common. I mean, you're practically the same person. At first, it freaked me out, but once he explained it, I understood."

I stared at our distorted reflection in the screen.

"So...have you ever felt that way about him?"

I avoided his gaze because I wasn't certain of my answer. My dreams had been pretty explicit for the past week. There was no doubt I was attracted to him. The second his shirt came off, my mind was in the gutter. But I'd been around him my whole life and never felt that way before. Why did I feel differently now? "No."

"Oh..." Rex didn't hide his disappointment.

Even if I did have deep feelings for Zeke, I would never admit it. He was with Rochelle now, and the last thing I would ever do was ruin something good for him. All I felt was an attraction and nothing more.

At least I hoped.

Ray of Love

Chapter Six

Rae

All I could think about was Zeke.

Knowing he had feelings for me was a really big deal. It made me question my own perception about our friendship. My best friend digging me should have been something I picked up on. Thankfully, only Rex and I knew about it. If Kayden and Jessie did too, it would be really difficult for me to pretend everything was normal.

"Zeke is coming over. Just to give you a heads-up."

"Why?" It came out defensive and rude, but the damage was done. "I mean, what are you guys doing?"

"I'm not sure yet. We might go out. We might stay here."

"And Rochelle?" I couldn't tell if I wanted her to be there or not. A part of me wanted her there so I wouldn't feel guilty for spending time with him. But I also didn't want her there because I would really feel guilty anytime I was around her.

"No. Just him." Rex grabbed a beer from the fridge and popped off the cap. "Why?"

"Just want to be prepared."

"You know, you don't have to make it weird."

"I'm not," I snapped. "Everything is the same."

"Then why are your cheeks red, you can't stand still, and your eyes look like they're about to pop out of your head?"

"Oh god, I really look like that?" I walked to the mirror hanging near the entryway and saw that he was right. But I didn't have time to calm down because Zeke knocked on the door then stepped inside.

"The coolest person in the world has arrived," Zeke announced as he walked in.

"Dude, the coolest person in the world was already here," Rex said. "He lives here."

Zeke set the case of beer he brought over onto the counter. "Wasn't sure if we were going out or not, but I thought I'd bring this just in case." He pulled the bottles out of the sleeves and set them on the counter. "What's up?"

"Nothing much," Rex said. "Just being cool."

"Break up with Bonnie?"

Rex noticeably tensed. "Yeah...it went pretty well."

"Who's Bonnie?" I blurted. He never mentioned that name to me. And he broke up with her? Wouldn't that mean he was in a relationship with her to begin with?

Zeke turned around because he didn't realize I was there. Beforehand, I had been standing behind the door. "Hey, Rae. Didn't see you." He crossed the room and enveloped his arms around me for a hug.

We hardly ever hugged, so I didn't know where the affection came from. I wanted to dart out of his grasp because the touch wasn't what it used to be. All I could think about were the naughty dreams I had about him. The image of him shirtless was ingrained in my mind forever. And now that he had a girlfriend, I felt like a tramp. "Uh...what's that for?"

He held me tightly against his chest, his rock-hard body feeling like a slab of concrete. When he took a breath, I could feel the expansion right against me. He smelled like cologne and pine needles, reminding me of his beautiful house near the coast. He was warm, his natural body heat protecting him from the cold outside. The fabric of his shirt was unbelievably soft against my skin, and an image of me wearing it to bed came to mind.

What the hell was wrong with me?

"Rochelle told me what you did." He pulled away so we could look at each other, but his hands were still tight around my waist. His fingers felt enormous against my frame, and I realized it was exactly how I pictured it would feel in my fantasies.

"What did I do?"

"My friends from college were dicks to her...and you had her back. I really appreciate that,

Rae." His eyes softened as he looked into mine. Those crystal blue eyes held unconditional affection, and I wanted to dive headfirst into that deep abyss. His hard jaw was covered in a bit of stubble, and the masculine curves of his face were beautiful in a manly way. I understood why all the girls liked him, but now the realization hit me hard.

"It wasn't a big deal...any woman would have done the same thing." No woman should ever let another feel objectified like that. To be mocked for not being a size zero was ridiculous, and those standards should be eradicated.

"No, they wouldn't." His hands moved around my waist, resting right under my ribs. "You're a good friend, Rae. I'm really lucky to have you."

I wanted to swoon right then and there. Every time I took a breath, I felt my stomach rise and press against his thumbs. I felt petite in his embrace, even safe. My heart was out of control, and my breathing was just as bad. Zeke did incredible things to me, things that I didn't even feel with Ryker.

What was going on?

He just thanked me for defending his girlfriend.

His girlfriend.

Get a hold of yourself, Rae. "I love Rochelle. I'd do anything for her. If you love her, I love her. And I'm happy that you have her." The words tumbled out like an avalanche, pouring out and spilling all over the floor. I spoke so quickly I wasn't even sure if I made sense. I was a mess, out of it and sounding like a lunatic. "Don't even worry about it."

"I know you do." He gave me a gentle squeeze. "She loves you too."

She wouldn't if she knew what I was thinking.

I had to get his hands off me. I felt guilty for just letting him touch me. "I've got to pee..." I dashed out of his embrace and headed down the hallway as fast as I could without running. I had to get away—and get away fast.

I got into the bathroom and sat on the lid of the toilet, finally feeling safe. I crossed my legs and crossed my arms over my chest, feeling my stomach lurch in painful ways. My waist still burned from where he rested his fingers.

Zeke's voice came from the kitchen. "Is she all right? Seems a little off today."

Rex responded. "She's always off, man. I wouldn't read too much into it."

At least Rex covered my ass. I made an idiot out of myself. He obviously thought the exact same thing.

***

Rex and Zeke took turns playing a video game, and at around two in the morning, Rex fell asleep on the couch. His head was against the armrest, and his mouth was open, spreading drool everywhere.

Zeke glanced at him when he heard him snore. "Lame." He finished the game and drove his car over the finish line. "First again." He handed the controller to me.

"I'm tired."

"You're lame too." He turned off the game and turned on the TV instead.

I sat on the opposite end of the couch, my knees pulled to my chest as I tried to keep my body away from his as much as possible. "Yep. That's me, Ms. Lame. So...Rex was seeing someone?"

"Some chick named Bonnie."

"I've never heard him mention her."

"They weren't serious. Just a fling that lasted a few months."

"A few months?" I forced myself to keep my voice low so Rex wouldn't wake up. "Who has a fling for three months?"

"That's what I said. I suggested he break it off before the poor girl gets hurt."

"Did she?"

"He made it sound like she was fine with it."

I yanked on the blanket hanging over the back of the couch and pulled it across my lap. "I can't picture any girl getting upset over Rex."

"Because you find him disgusting. I can't keep track of how many girls have come up to me and asked if he was available."

"Because they knew you weren't."

He looked at me, both eyebrows raised. "What?"

I realized what I said when it was far too late. "Because they knew you would know."

Zeke still seemed confused, but he shook it off. "Yeah, I think most people know we're close once they meet us."

It was hard to picture a time when he was single because it seemed like Rochelle had been around for a long time. In reality, it'd only been about six months. She was a cute fit for him. But now I kept picturing the time when he was available. All those nights he wanted to go home with me, and I could have made my dreams a reality whenever I wanted.

But that ship had sailed.

"So...is Rochelle feeling better?" I'd never forget the sight of her tears under the lamppost outside. She was devastated by the horrific things they said, and I couldn't blame her. They were cold, superficial, and mean.

"She is now. For a few days, she was still upset. I knew something was wrong. She was skipping all her meals and seemed down all the time. Eventually, I pulled the truth out of her."

"I'm sorry..."

"I gave those assholes a piece of my mind."

"What did you do?"

"I stopped by their apartments, and when they opened the doors, I slugged them each hard in the face. Then I left. I didn't even say a word."

"They deserved it."

"They deserved worse. I couldn't believe they actually said that shit the second she turned her back, especially with you standing there."

I shrugged. "Must have assumed I was an asshole too."

"It took me awhile to talk some reason into her. She may not be super skinny, but she's perfect the way she is. There's no need for her to change."

I loved the way he defended her. It even made me smile. But then I felt guilt all over again because my attraction grew. Zeke was a gorgeous man who could have whoever he wanted, but he never saw himself that way. He was humble about his appearance, his intelligence, and everything else. He looked at women as people, not objects. "There's not."

"And I like her curves. I think I make it pretty clear every night that I love her body."

And now I felt a little sick.

Picturing him having sex with her just made me feel light-headed. Even thinking about him kissing her was painful. After the way he hugged me, it was difficult to imagine him hugging anyone else. This sense of entitlement and impropriety came out of nowhere. "I'm sure she'll forget the whole thing eventually."

"Yeah, hopefully." He turned down the volume of the TV then leaned against the back of the couch. "So, seeing anyone?"

"No." There was only one man I was seeing in my dreams. I hadn't even been using my vibrator because I didn't need it. My subconscious thoughts took care of all my needs. "Not a soul." I felt my cheeks burn slightly.

"When we went out the other night, all the guys were looking at you."

"They were looking at Jessie."

"No. You."

I didn't notice. "That's nice of you to say, but I don't need an ego boost. That's not the problem."

"Then what is the problem?"

"I guess I wasn't ready."

"Wasn't?" he asked. "Are you ready now?"

My sex dreams about Zeke were the first indication that I was ready for a physical relationship with someone new. Before that, I had absolutely no mojo, and whatever romantic dreams I did have were usually about Ryker. "I'm more open to the idea..."

"Maybe I could set you up with someone."

"No!"

Both of his eyebrows shot up.

"I mean...that's okay." Zeke was the last person I wanted to set me up.

"Are you sure? Rochelle has a few good guy friends. One of them is pretty handsome. He's a pro golfer."

"A golfer? I want someone my age."

"He is our age," he said with a chuckle. "He's a good guy. Got out of a serious relationship about a year ago. He's taken some time to get back on his feet."

"I really don't think that's a good idea—"

"It's settled. I'll talk to him."

"Zeke, don't—"

"Just go on one date. It probably won't go anywhere, but it's a good way to get your feet in the water. We'll make it a double date. That way it won't feel too serious."

A double date? Are you kidding me? "I think I'll pass."

"Too bad." He turned back to the TV like the conversation was over.

"Why are you pushing me so much?" Why did he care if I was seeing someone or not? When he did have feelings for me, he never tried to stop my dates, and he never seemed particularly interested in what I did romantically. But now, he was butting in like Jessie or Kayden.

"Because I remember how happy you were with him." He didn't say his name, and it was obviously intentional. "And I want you to be happy again. Isn't that all a friend really wants? For their friends to be happy?"

***

"I can't believe I'm doing this..." I wore a short black dress with heels, and Jessie helped with my hair and makeup. When the gang realized I was going on my first date since Ryker, they acted like parents whose oldest child was going to prom.

"You'll be fine," Zeke said. "Just be yourself. I can promise you, this guy is going to take one look at you and think he hit the jackpot. And when you open your mouth and show him who you really are, he's going to think he's the luckiest guy in the world."

It was such a sweet thing to say, and for a second, I forgot I was on a date with someone else because I was too busy staring into Zeke's beautiful eyes. "That's nice of you to say."

"I mean it." He placed his hand in the center of my back, his warm touch nearly burning me. "Rae, you're the most desirable woman on the planet. You could have any guy you want. Even if this guy is kinda famous, he's going to think you're out of his league."

"Zeke…stop."

"I'm just telling you how it is." He gave me a gentle pat before he dropped his hand.

Rochelle returned from the bathroom, wearing a champagne pink dress. Her blonde hair was curled and pulled over one shoulder. The second she walked away, I forgot about her. It seemed like Zeke and I were the only two people enjoying the evening.

That was terrible.

We entered the restaurant and took our seats at a table in the corner. My date was already there, wearing a collared shirt and a black tie. In my head, I pictured a man in his late thirties that was ridiculously tanned. His eyes permanently squinted from being in the sun all day long.

But he looked nothing like that.

He was young, probably my age. When he smiled, a dimple formed in each cheek. He had short brown hair and brilliant green eyes. He immediately rose to his feet when we reached the table, and the glance-over he gave me told me he liked what he saw. "Wow...I'm one lucky man." He shook my hand. "Owen."

"Rae."

He pulled out the chair for me. "It's a pleasure to meet you."

We took our seats, and I felt my date stare at me with pure intensity. He was really handsome and fit, my type exactly. His skin was kissed by the sun and contained a healthy glow. His shoulders were broad and powerful, and he carried himself with a masculine posture.

But all I could do was look at Zeke.

He leaned toward Rochelle and shared a quiet whisper. She smiled in return then they shared the wine list as they decided what to get. They didn't make conversation with us, probably giving us time to get to know one another.

"Rochelle tells me you're an analytical chemist. That's impressive."

"That's just a fancy word for nerd," I said with a chuckle.

He chuckled in response. "Still impressive all the same. What do you do exactly?"

I told him about my work at COLLECT.

"That's very cool. And important."

"So you play golf?" I realized how amateur I made it seem. "I mean, you're a professional golfer?"

He didn't seem offended by the way I downplayed it. "Yeah. I've been doing it for about two years now. Started right out of college. I really love it. I get to travel to beautiful places, and I've met some of my idols along the way. Just a few weeks ago, I met Tiger Woods."

"Seriously?" I asked. "That's so cool."

"Do you watch golf?"

"No..." I didn't want to lie and then get caught later. "I follow basketball and football. But I like sports in general."

"That's cool. As long as you have an appreciation for sports in general, I think we'll be just fine." He winked.

I smiled back then looked at Zeke again. He was talking to Rochelle about his day at work. He didn't pay any attention to us, and his eyes were entirely focused on her. It seemed like we weren't even there.

And for some reason, that made me feel empty inside.

***

The four of us walked to the parking lot together, in pairs.

"Can I take you home?" Owen walked beside me, his hand in his pocket as he towered over me with his height.

I immediately glanced at Zeke and Rochelle. Zeke's arm was around her waist, and they were chuckling together, having a good time and not caring about the two of us. I wanted Zeke to take me home, but I knew they would probably head to his place right away. I didn't want to slow down their evening. "Yeah, sure."

We reached the parking lot then said goodnight.

"I'm going to take Rae home," Owen said. "Have a good night."

"Sure thing." Zeke walked to me then hugged me, but it was just an excuse to get close to me. "Are you okay with that? Because I don't mind taking you home."

Now that I was in his arms with his lips near my ear, I never wanted to let go. I could stay like that forever and feel safe until the end of time. "No. That's not necessary."

"Are you sure?" he whispered.

"Yeah. Have a good night." Despite how incredible he felt and smelled, I had to get away from him. His lover was standing just five feet away, and I had a nice guy waiting for me. I shouldn't have been focusing on Zeke at all. "See you later."

I got into the car with Owen, and he drove to my apartment just a few blocks away. He got out of the car and walked me to my door on the fourth floor. His hands remained in his pockets, so it didn't seem like he intended to make any moves on me. When Cameron walked me home, he pushed me against the door and stuck his tongue up my nose.

Not exactly hot.

"This is me." I stopped in front of the door and turned to him.

His eyes contained his hope, wanting me to invite him inside.

Not gonna happen. "Thank you for dinner and spending the evening with me."

He quickly hid his disappointment when he realized he wasn't getting what he wanted. "Of course. The pleasure was entirely mine."

He had everything I was looking for. He was polite, smart, and easy-going. Under different circumstances, I'd probably invite him inside. But the action didn't feel right at all. All I could think about was Zeke, even though he was spending his evening with Rochelle.

His girlfriend.

"Maybe we can go out again sometime?" Owen asked hopefully.

I wanted to let this guy down gently because there was absolutely nothing wrong with him. The problem was me. "You're a really nice guy, Owen. I've enjoyed spending time with you. But this evening has just made me realize I'm not ready to date yet. Honestly, it has nothing to do with you. If I were in a better place, I'm sure this would have gone quite differently."

He took the rejection well. "I understand. It took me almost a year before I was finally in a place where I could really be with another woman and feel good about it. Rochelle mentioned you've been single for a few months now. Maybe you just need more time."

"Thanks for being so understanding..."

"Of course. I just hope you'll do something for me."

"Sure."

"If you're ever in that place again, give me a call. I'd love to go out again, even if it's in a few months."

The request actually made me smile. "Of course."

"Great." He shook my hand then gave me a nod. "I hope we see each other again." He walked away and headed down the hallway. Instead of taking the elevator, he took the stairs, probably so he wouldn't have to look at me as he waited for the doors to close.

I opened my door and walked inside.

Rex was standing at the counter, and judging by how guilty he looked, he was just eavesdropping. He stirred a glass of water with a spoon, pretending he was doing something that justified him being in the kitchen and right next to the door.

"Growing sea monkeys?"

"What?" he asked with a nervous laugh. "Just making a protein shake."

"Really? Because it looks like you're just stirring a glass of water."

"No..." He stirred it harder before he tossed the spoon in the sink. "So...how'd your date go?"

"Don't act like you weren't listening, Rex. I'm not stupid."

He dropped the act once he knew he'd been caught. "What was wrong with him? I Googled the guy, and he's smoking hot."

I tossed my purse on the counter and gave him a look full of concern. "Excuse me?"

"And he's a great golfer. He's actually pretty wealthy."

"You know me, Rex. I don't care about money. I can take care of myself just fine."

"That's not how I meant it, and you know it. I'm just saying this guy was a catch. Tell me one bad thing about him."

"There's nothing bad about him." I leaned against the counter and slipped off my heels.

"Then why aren't you seeing him again?"

I tossed my shoes by the door and finally stood on the tile, feeling relieved by the touch of the flat surface. "I just don't think I'm ready to be dating."

"It's been three months. I thought you were over him."

"I am." Ryker wasn't the problem. He was finally out of my head and a ghost of the past. Even when I saw him at the funeral, I didn't feel the way I used to.

"Then help me understand this."

143

Zeke popped into my head. I pictured his adorable smile and the sexy way he smoldered without even realizing it. I imagined him shirtless on the basketball court. I remembered the way he took care of me when I was hung over. And I remembered that thoughtful gift he gave me for my birthday. My heart sunk with heaviness, and I suddenly felt defeated—like I'd never be happy again. "It just wasn't right. That's all."

Rex sighed in annoyance.

"You used to hate it when I dated, and now you're anxious for me to bring a guy home."

"I'm not anxious for you to have a boyfriend. I'm anxious for you to be happy. That's all."

My eyes softened. "I am happy, Rex."

"Not like you were before."

"Well, I was in love at the time. Of course I was happy."

"Well, be in love again. But with the right guy."

Again, I thought of Zeke. "Believe me, I want that more than you do."

"Then keep dating until you find Mr. Right."

"Maybe I already found Mr. Right, but he's not available..."

"What?" he asked blankly.

"Nothing." I wasn't even sure why I said that. "So, when are you moving out?" It was the first thing that came to mind, and I blurted it out.

"Soon. By the way..." He grabbed his wallet off the counter and pulled a check out. "I'm halfway there." He handed it to me.

I looked at the check and saw the total for half of my investment. "Wow. That was fast."

"I'm telling you, I'm frugal as well. But look where it got me." He pointed to the check. "You and Zeke are both almost paid up. I just need another month or so, and we'll be square."

"And then you'll move out?"

"Shut up. You know you'll miss me when I'm gone."

"I really, really won't."

"Whatever. This apartment is going to be so quiet with just the two of you."

"Two of us?" As in, me and someone else? Like Zeke?

"Yeah. You and Safari."

"Oh...yeah." Seriously, what was wrong with me?

Rex tilted his head as he examined me, knowing something was off. "For some reason, I feel like something is up. I can't explain why or how...but I just know."

"Nothing is up. You're wrong."

"No...I can still see it." He narrowed his gaze on my eyes. "I'm missing something, but I don't know what."

"You're just a paranoid weirdo. That's what." I grabbed my purse off the counter and walked to my bedroom. "Good night, Rex."

"You're going to bed?" he called after me. "It's 9:30."

"No. I just want to get away from you." And fall asleep as quickly as possible. Maybe I would have a good dream tonight...

Chapter Seven

Rex

"I can't believe Rae didn't want to see him again." I dropped three slices onto my plate and took an enormous bite of the crust first. "That guy is a total chick magnet."

Zeke shrugged. "I don't get it either. They seemed to have a good time, and he was really into her. When he told Rochelle about it, he seemed pretty down."

"Not sure why..."

"Come on, Rex. You know why." He dropped the jalapenos on his pizza before he took a bite. "Why do you always eat the crust first? So weird..."

"It's better that way," I said defensively. "Who puts jalapenos on their pizza?"

"Lots of people..."

"More like weirdos." I finished my first slice and had grease all over my hands since I held on to the edge of the pizza rather than the crust.

"Have you talked to Bonnie?"

I moved on to my second slice. "Who?"

"Bonnie? That girl you were seeing."

Oh yeah. I drank my soda to clear my throat. "Actually, no. She hasn't called or anything. And I haven't seen her around."

"So either she took it well, or she's really pissed."

"No, she's not pissed." Kayden would tell me if she felt otherwise. "I'm sure I'll see her around and everything will be fine. We both knew our booty call situation had an expiration date."

"Have you slept with anyone since?"

"No...but it's only been a week. Haven't really had the time to meet women."

"Yeah, true."

"Why are you so obsessed with my love life, man?"

150

"Obsessed?" He finished a slice then wiped his fingers on a napkin. "Just curious. It's not like you aren't obsessed with mine."

Now that Rae knew how he used to feel about her, it'd definitely become more interesting. But unfortunately, Rae didn't take the bait. It made me realize that Zeke never really had a shot with her. Settling down with Rochelle was the best thing for him. I probably shouldn't have said anything to begin with. "Getting nervous?"

"For what?"

"Proposing? You know, the scariest shit a man can do."

"Oh, that. Not really. I already have everything planned out. All I have to do is go for it."

"When is this happening?"

"In about three weeks. I think she'll love it."

"Shit, I would love it." A moonlight dinner on a yacht...can't beat that.

"Then I'm going to ask her to move in with me right away. I don't see the point in waiting until we actually get married. Not much point in me having that big house if I'm the only one who lives in it."

"Then why did you buy it?" I asked with a laugh.

He shrugged. "I knew I would shack up with a hottie someday. Besides, the chicks dig my pad. It'll be a good way to convince Rochelle to say yes if she's on the fence about marrying me."

"That's ridiculous, Zeke. She's going to scream at the top of her lungs and beg you to marry her right then and there."

He smiled. "You think so?"

"Come on, you know you're hot."

He clapped me on the shoulder. "Thanks, man."

I cleared my throat. "Eh-hem."

"Oh, and you're hot too."

"Thank you."

"I'm glad Rochelle didn't hear that conversation. Then she really would consider saying no."

"Nah," I said with a chuckle. "She would just think you're bi."

***

The longer I went without talking to Kayden, the more out of place I felt. It was weird not telling her about my day or a great joke I heard, and it was weird not getting any action on a regular basis.

My life started to feel worthless.

I didn't know what to do with my spare time, and since I had nowhere to go, I stayed at the apartment with Rae a lot more often—which sucked. I caught myself typing a message to Kayden only to realize I probably shouldn't do that anymore.

We were still friends, of course. But we weren't that kind of friends anymore. I couldn't text her whenever I wanted just because I missed her.

And I did miss her.

I decided to go by the library on my lunch break, an excuse to see her. She hadn't been out with the group, so I hadn't bumped into her since our booty call situation came to an end. I didn't want to make it obvious I was just trying to see her. But not seeing her at all seriously bummed me out.

I walked inside and past the front desk. A few women were working the computers, and another was stacking returned books on a cart with wheels. After a quick scan, I realized Kayden wasn't there. I walked to the first worker I saw. "Hey, is Kayden around today?"

"No," she said. "She called in sick this week. I guess she came down with the flu."

"Oh…" I didn't have a clue she was sick. "Thanks."

***

I went by Panera and picked up a cup of soup before I headed to her apartment. No wonder why she hadn't been around. I didn't have a clue she was under the weather. It wouldn't hurt to bring her soup, right? No harm in that.

I knocked on the door but there wasn't an answer.

I knocked again. "Kayden? It's Rex." I held the brown paper bag in my hands and listened to the sound of light feet as they headed to the door. The locks clicked as they were undone and the door swung inward.

She definitely looked ill. Her face was pale like white paint, and her cheeks were hollow like she hadn't been drinking enough fluids. Her hair was in a messy bun, and her pajamas looked too many sizes too big. "Rex...what are you doing here?"

I held up the bag. "The girls at the library said you were sick. So I thought I'd bring you some soup."

"Oh..." Instead of being happy to see me, she nearly looked repulsed. "Why were you there?"

"I had to pick up a book. When I didn't see you, I asked where you were."

155

"Oh..."

Normally, I would just walk in, but the relationship was different now. "So...can I come in?"

"Uh...my apartment is a mess right now. And it's an incubator for bacteria." She took the bag out of my hands. "It was nice of you to bring this for me. Thanks." She kept one hand on the door like she would block my way if I tried to go inside.

"You're welcome. I'm sorry you're sick."

"It's okay...it'll go away soon." Her eyes had bags underneath, and even though she didn't wear any makeup, her eyes looked unusually dark and sunken in. "Well, thank you. I'll see you around." Without waiting for me to say goodbye, she shut the door in my face.

I didn't appreciate the cold shoulder, but before I could be offended, I remembered she was the one who was under the weather. If I were really sick, I wouldn't want to entertain anyone either.

So I went home.

Chapter Eight

Rae

"Let's hit the court." Zeke spun the basketball on his forefinger then waggled his eyebrows at the same time. "The Monstars versus The Toonsquad."

"Rex isn't home."

"Just us—one-on-one. Like we always do."

I didn't want to do anything one-on-one with him. The dreams were getting worse, and my waking thoughts weren't improving either. Every day was getting harder than the last, and I felt a transformation slowly taking place. I could hardly look at Zeke the way I used to. He used to just be my good friend Zeke.

But now he was *Zeke*.

Hunky.

Dreamy.

Sexy.

Sweet.

And goddamn perfect.

Who was taken.

I had to keep reminding myself he was crazy about Rochelle—not me.

"I'm kinda tired… I think I'm gonna take a nap." I wanted him out of my apartment—pronto. It didn't feel appropriate having him around when no one else was there to supervise us. We used to hang out alone all the time, but now I felt like a conniving little skank.

Because my thoughts weren't pure whatsoever.

If some woman wanted my man and she was hanging out with him all the time, I wouldn't exactly be a fan of it. And all I could think about was Rochelle…that sweet woman who was perfect for him in ways I would never be.

Such a betrayal.

"A nap?" he asked with a laugh. "It's five. You usually go to bed at ten."

"What can I say? I'm lazy."

He burst out with a laugh. "Yeah…okay."

"What? I am."

"You're the least lazy person I know. You make Taylor Swift look unmotivated."

"Thank you for comparing me to Taylor Swift because you know I love her, and I'm a Swifty and everything...but I'm just not feeling it."

"Come on. Safari needs to go out anyway."

Would he just get off my ass? "Fine, okay."

"Yes!"

***

Safari lay just behind the pole and watched us play on the court.

I couldn't get into the game because I forced myself to stay at least five feet away from him the entire time. Thankfully, it was a cold day, so he had to keep his shirt on.

Every time he moved around me, I let him pass. He scored, and then I got the ball back. But when he blocked me, he had no problem touching my arm or shoulder. And every time he did, I shuddered with guilt because I actually liked it.

So he stole the ball from me four times.

Which was just embarrassing.

After he made a shot, he tucked the ball under his arm and stared me down. "What's gotten into you?"

"Me? What are you talking about?"

"You totally suck today. And you never suck, Rae."

That's not true. I sucked, and I sucked good. And I wouldn't mind proving it to him.

Goddammit, I'm going to hell. When I reached the pearly gates, God would wave his finger at me in shame and send me straight down below.

And I wouldn't argue because I deserved it.

"I told you, I'm just tired."

"Even when you're tired, you're better than this. Let's step it up." He set the ball down then pulled his shirt over his head.

No. No. No.

Why are you doing this to me?

Stop! Now!

"You've got to be kidding me…"

"What?" He turned around and dribbled the ball as he walked toward me, his perfect body bulging with tight and lean muscle. His pecs were each the size of a Frisbee, and his shoulders were so smooth with sculpted muscle he looked like a statue. His slender waist was ripped with his abdominals, and a noticeable V disappeared into his shorts.

I bit my bottom lip on accident, but I quickly released it when I realized just how ridiculous I was being. "I told you to hurry up so we could finish this game."

He accepted the explanation without question. Thankfully.

We started up the game again, but then I sucked even more. I kept a greater distance between us, not wanting him anywhere near me with his hot and sweaty body. If I could've held my hands up like I was being frisked, I would've.

In one instance, I had him pinned in the corner so it was difficult for him to make a shot. He tried to find the right angle to land the ball in the hoop, but he was stuck. I eyed the ball as he held it to the side of his chest, both of his hands on it.

And then I did something totally inappropriate.

Totally wrong.

Unacceptable.

And skanky.

I pretended to go for the ball but I purposely touched his chest, running my hand from his pecs to his stomach.

Jesus Christ.

Perfection.

Sweaty, muscled, goddamn perfection.

He maneuvered around me and shot the ball, making it in and bringing his score to a zillion points higher than mine.

But I didn't care that I lost.

I didn't care about anything anymore.

Because I had bigger problems than losing a stupid basketball game.

Much bigger problems.

***

"You can't tell anyone this. I mean it. Not a goddamn soul."

Jessie sat across from me at the table with her drink resting on a coaster. She didn't care about her large glass of alcohol because my topic of conversation was much more interesting. "Girl, just tell me!"

"You have to promise me."

"Fine. I promise. When have I ever told your secrets to anyone?"

Never. Because best friends didn't do that shit.

"What about Kayden?" she asked. "Don't you want to tell her too?"

"I texted her, but she said she was sick. I guess she's got a serious bug or something. Haven't seen her in over a week now."

"Okay, I guess I'm the only one who gets this delicious piece of news." She rubbed her palms together excitedly. "Come on, spill it already. I know this is going to be big. You never make me promise to be quiet."

This was big. I didn't even know where to start.

She leaned forward. "Come on...you can do it."

"I don't even know where to begin. I'm not sure when it happened or how it happened..."

"Just tell me!" She slammed her fists on the table and shook her drink.

"You're going to think I'm a slut."

"Girl, I wish you were more of a slut."

"Okay...you're right."

"So just say whatever pops into your mind." She snapped her fingers. "Go."

"Okay...so a few weeks ago, I started to..."

She leaned forward more.

"Look at Zeke differently. I'm not sure when it happened or how, but I—"

"Shut your face!" She covered her mouth with her hands and screamed. "This is huge!"

"Will you let me finish?"

"I'll try." She fanned her face like she was about to melt.

"I started having these dreams about him. Like...sexual dreams."

She covered her mouth again, but this time she hid her scream.

"We were playing basketball together one day and he took off his shirt and...I guess it got my engine revving."

She screamed into her hand.

"And then he got me that nice gift, and he's always around all the time. And then...you really have to keep this to yourself, okay?"

"You have even bigger news?"

"Yeah. Rochelle told me Zeke used to have feelings for me before they dated."

She threw her hands on the table again. "Oh. My. Fucking. God."

"And I haven't been able to look at him as a friend ever since. Anytime I'm near him, I'm picturing him naked or how his kiss would feel. And these damn dreams just won't go away. And Rochelle...I feel so bad. He has a girlfriend, and I can't stop thinking about him like this. Jessie, help me."

"Help you what?"

"Tell me this is just a really weird crush and it'll go away. It'll go away, right?" I needed to hear that right now. Otherwise, I was doomed.

"Well...are the dreams purely sexual?"

"I think so."

"Are they romantic? Are you going on dates? Is he telling you he loves you?"

A guilty look stretched across my face.

"Oh shit..."

I knew what my answer was.

"It doesn't sound purely physical, Rae. I'm sorry..."

I covered my face. "No...this is a nightmare."

"I can't believe this." She ran her hand through her hair anxiously. "You guys would be the cutest couple ever."

"Jess, he has a girlfriend."

"But she won't be around forever."

"Are you kidding me? This is the longest I've ever seen him stay with the same woman. And we all love her."

"Well, of course," Jessie said. "Rochelle is great. Don't get me wrong. But come on, you guys make way more sense."

"How do you figure? She's a doctor just like Zeke. They have everything in common. I can't compete with that, and I don't want to."

"How long did his feelings for you last?"

I remembered everything Rex said from our conversation because it was such big news. "On and off for about three years."

Jessie's jaw dropped. "Three years...three?"

I nodded. "That's what he said."

"No one has feelings for someone for three years," she shrieked. "He didn't just have a crush on you. He was straight up in love with you."

"We don't know that..."

"It's so obvious. When did he get over you?"

"Apparently, he was going to ask me out right before I started seeing Ryker."

"And that wasn't even that long ago. I bet he still feels the same way."

I knew that wasn't possible. "He's head over heels for Rochelle. It's obvious he doesn't think about me that way."

"No." She held up her hand. "If you love someone for three years, those feelings don't just go away. He probably only moved on because he knew he couldn't get you."

"And I would agree with you if he hadn't been seeing Rochelle for so long. When have you seen Zeke with a girl for more than three weeks?"

Jessie's face fell slack.

"Never. They tell each other they love each other. And they've met each other's parents. If that's not serious, I don't know what is."

Jessie didn't have an argument against that.

"I think I missed my chance."

"If these feelings are serious, I think you should tell him."

"God, no. Never."

"Why the hell not? He should know."

"I'm not messing things up with Rochelle. He could have told me how he felt when I was seeing Ryker but he didn't. Like I wouldn't give him the same respect."

She sighed in defeat. "But this is different..."

"Doesn't matter. And I wouldn't do that to Rochelle. She's a great person."

"I know she is..."

"And even if I did tell him, he probably wouldn't feel the same way, and I would just make our friendship awkward. We would never be the same after that. And if Rochelle knew I was into him, she wouldn't want him to see me anymore. No one would blame her. And then I would lose Zeke altogether."

She shrugged in agreement. "Then what are you going to do?"

"I don't know. Get over him, I guess."

"Well, you dumped that golfer so you're off to a good start..."

"I don't have to date someone to get over him. I'll just avoid him."

"If Rex wasn't living with you, I would say that's possible. But since he is, you're screwed."

I knew she was right. "I guess I need to get rid of him."

"Pronto."

"You won't believe what I did when we were playing ball the other day...something slutty."

"I'll be the judge of that." She beckoned me with her fingers. "Lay it on me."

"He had the ball, and I was blocking him. So I pretended to go for the ball and purposely dragged my hand down his chest and over his abs. And day-yum it was nice." I covered one eye in shame.

Jessie shook her head. "I hate it to say it, but...that was really slutty."

"I know."

"You definitely need some space."

"Yeah..."

"And if you can't get it, you should lie and say you have a conference or something. Give yourself a week or two to clear your head."

"That's not a bad idea."

"And use your vibrator until he's out of your system for good."

It was all charged up and ready to go.

***

"I need you to move out." I grabbed the remote and turned off the TV.

He was in the middle of watching a game, and he wasn't happy about the privilege being revoked. "What?"

"You've been here long enough. I think it's time we both had our own space. I know you're making good money now, so you can afford it."

"But—"

"I don't even care if you pay me back at this point." I tossed the list of vacant apartments and houses on the table. "I've done all the research for you. The best ones are at the top, and the worst ones are at the bottom. They're all in your price range and close to work. So get on it and figure it out."

He grabbed the papers and browsed through them. "If you just give me two months, I'll be debt free."

"How much do you think rent is? You're only saving like four thousand bucks, Rex. Just go for it."

"But I have to furnish the apartment. In case you forgot, I had to sell all my things just to make rent for the bowling alley. I don't have a bed, a couch, or even plates. I literally don't have anything. It's going to cost a lot more than four thousand dollars. I didn't realize I was annoying you so bad that you felt the need to do this." He held up the papers then tossed them back on the table.

Now I felt bad. "You aren't annoying me..."

"Then what's the problem?"

"I just..." For a second, I actually considered telling him the truth. He knew how Zeke felt about me in the past. But then I decided against it. "Never mind."

"Rae, what's up?" he pressed. "Because you're being weird, and when you're being weird, it usually means something is up."

"Nothing...just that time of the month."

That shut him up real quick. He grabbed the remote and turned the TV back on, doing his best to pretend that awkward sentence didn't enter his delicate ears.

"Anyway, I'm actually leaving for a conference tomorrow. I won't be back for a few weeks."

"A conference?" he asked. "Where?"

I made up a place on the spot. "New York. While I'm there, I'm going to do some sightseeing so I won't be back for at least ten days."

"That's far. Is Ryker going?"

"No. It's just for Jenny and me."

"That's pretty cool. Free trip. And great for me because I'll finally have some peace and quiet."

"Yep." And I'll have time to forget about Zeke. "I'm leaving tomorrow. You're in charge of Safari."

"First, you tell me to move out, and now you're leaving?"

"I was hoping you'd be gone by the time I got back."

He bought it. "Oh."

"So, I'll see you in ten days."

"You need help with anything? Packing? Lift to the airport?"

"You don't own a car, Rex."

"Oh yeah...but I can Uber with you."

"Nah. My flight leaves in the morning. You'll still be asleep."

"True."

***

I checked in to the cheapest room I could find at the hotel right beside my work. It was a little expensive, but I didn't spend my money on much anyway. And I really needed a break from my life.

And Zeke.

If I spent some time by myself and tried to be objective, I was sure I could squash this little crush. Whatever my feelings were for Zeke, they were only superficial and temporary. Maybe I only wanted him because I was surprised he ever wanted me.

There was a logical explanation.

And these feelings would go away.

I went to work in the morning and then returned to my hotel like clockwork. At first, it was exciting because I finally had some space to myself. I didn't have to see Rex sitting on my couch the second I walked through the door. I could walk around in my underwear and watch whatever I wanted on TV.

But the excitement wore off after a few days.

Quickly, I started to feel lonely and isolated.

And worst of all, my feelings for Zeke were only getting worse. Not being around him made me miss him. When something remotely interesting happened in my life, I wanted to tell him about it. I wanted to go play basketball, but then I realized I didn't have him to play with. And my dreams were just as vivid as ever.

I was eating the rest of my sandwich from lunch when Zeke called me.

I saw his name on the screen and nearly panicked.

Why was he calling me?

Did he know?

Ah!

I quickly swallowed my food then answered. "Heeey." I covered my eyes when I realized how stupid I sounded. Zeke turned my world upside down, and he made me so nervous that I acted like a complete dork.

"Hey. How's New York?" His deep voice came over the line, innately sexy and charming.

I could listen to that voice all day. "It's good. Conference is kinda boring but whatever."

"What's it about?"

"Recycling...biodegradable resources...new strains of bacteria..." I was pulling all of this out of my ass. It was hard to lie to a fellow scientist.

But Zeke didn't question it. "Cool. Done any sightseeing?"

"Jenny and I went to the MET yesterday. That was pretty cool."

"Awesome. Clubbing?"

"Not so much. I've been too tired in the evenings."

"I can only imagine. Your brain must want to explode."

I closed my eyes and pictured his face, realizing how much I missed him—and it'd only been four days. "What have you been up to?"

"Working a lot. We had a scheduling mishap, so I'm seeing twice as many patients with half the time I usually have."

"How'd that happen?"

"My secretary made a mistake with the software...but it's only for this week. Then I'll get my lunch breaks again."

"Working on an empty stomach...yikes."

"I know, right?" he asked with a chuckle.

The sexiest chuckle ever.

"Rochelle and I went to the movies last night, and then Rex and I went bowling today. That was cool."

When he mentioned Rochelle, I actually felt a twinge of jealousy.

Which was absolutely ridiculous.

"Sounds like you've been having just as much fun while I've been away."

"Not really." His voice became quiet, and he paused for so long I didn't think I'd get an elaboration. "I miss you."

I closed my eyes and held my breath, my entire body aching from the innocent thing he just said. He meant it platonically, being affectionate with someone he saw as a friend. But it meant so much more to me, made me read between the lines and hope there was more to those three simple words. "I miss you too..." I pulled my knees to my chest and opened my eyes, still feeling the distant ache.

"I have no one to play basketball with. I have no one to talk shit about Rex with. I have no one to get lunch with. My life is pretty empty without you, Rae."

He was torturing me. "I'm pretty lonely without you guys too."

"When are you coming back?"

"Not for another six days." Maybe even less since this distance plan wasn't working whatsoever.

"A whole other week?" He whistled. "Damn, that's a long time. I wonder if New York will still be standing by the time you leave."

"It was here long before I was. And it'll be here long after."

"Whatever you say, Rae. I'll let you go. I know it's late there."

Oh yeah. New York was three hours ahead. "Yeah, I should get to bed."

"Good night, Rae."

I loved it when he said my name. It sounded exactly the same as it did in my dreams. "Good night, Zeke."

***

A few days later, I walked to my hotel from work, traveling on foot because I was so close. My hotel room was no longer a safe haven because it was just an empty room void of people and friends.

I couldn't wait to go home.

And though I never thought I would say this, I missed Rex like crazy.

I wasn't over Zeke at all. In fact, I was even more hung up on him.

Why did he have to call me?

"Rae."

I was just about to open the door to the hotel when I recognized that unmistakable voice. It was deep and powerful, containing the authority of a man I knew intimately well. I hadn't seen him in months, and I hoped I wouldn't see him again.

I turned around and saw Ryker standing in front of the window, wearing a black suit with a long overcoat. He looked the same as always, his eyes sparkling blue with rage embedded deep inside. "Ryker."

He eyed the hotel before he returned his look to me. "I've seen you walk here every day after work. My curiosity has gotten the best of me."

My eyebrow immediately popped up with suspicion. "Why have you been watching me?"

He nodded toward the COLLECT building. "My office window faces this hotel. Don't worry, I haven't been spying. But I still want to know what you're doing, so I decided to ask."

"Not really any of your business to ask."

He didn't react to the insult. "Hooking up with a married man?"

I almost slapped him. "Excuse me?"

"Not your style, I know. But why are you sneaking off to a hotel every day?"

"Wow, you're nosy. And I'm not sneaking." I refused to answer his question, especially after the insult he just gave me.

"I'm sorry." He ran his hand through his hair, the remorse coming into his eyes. "We got off on the wrong foot. I didn't mean to come over here and insult you. Honestly, I've seen you every day, and I've been looking for an excuse to talk to you. Your life is obviously a lot more interesting than mine, and I'm curious. Did you buy a house and you're getting ready to move in?"

I knew when Ryker was sincere, and I could tell he didn't mean to anger me on purpose. "No. Rex is still living with me, and I...just needed some space."

"That guy makes money. Tell him to move out."

"He wants to wait a few more months to save money."

"Who knew he could be so frugal?"

"He wants to pay Zeke and me back first. At least he has good intentions."

"Always has." He put his hands in the pockets of his coat. "So...how have you been?"

"Good. Just work and living life." And trying to get over my best friend, who has a girlfriend.

"Have a good birthday?"

I was surprised he knew when I had a birthday. I never told him about it. "It was a lot of fun. How did you know?"

"Jenny mentioned something one day when I saw her in the copy room."

I still didn't know how I could have come up. "Getting older isn't any fun. But getting drunk is."

He chuckled. "Words we should all live by."

I chuckled at his charming sarcasm. "How are you?"

He knew exactly what I was asking because his eyes darkened in sadness. "You know...I'm..." He shrugged when he didn't have a full response.

I felt terrible for him.

He cleared his throat and changed the subject. "You want to get a drink? There's a pub just a block away."

I didn't think he was making a move on me. It wouldn't make any sense if he did. He was the one who dumped me, and he never showed any interest in getting back together. It must have been a friendly invitation. And that wasn't the worst thing in the world. We'd had enough time to get over our old relationship, and he was my boss. There was no reason we couldn't be civil to one another—and maybe even be friends. "Yeah, I've got some time." And I had cabin fever from spending every afternoon alone. Lately, I'd been chatting Jenny's ear off in the lab. I was pretty sure she was annoyed with me.

"Great."

***

We made small talk about work, sports, and the abnormally rainy season we'd been having. Ryker didn't mention our romance or talk about anyone he was seeing. I didn't want to know so I was glad the subject didn't come up. If I weren't over him and into

Zeke, this meeting would have been much more difficult.

"What's the gang been up to?" He drank an Old Fashioned, like usual. Some things never changed.

"Jessie is still at the hair salon. I really think she needs to open up her own studio. She has a talent for that sort of thing. And Kayden is still at the library. She's been sick for nearly two weeks—poor girl. Rex is...well, Rex." When I mentioned the last member of the group, I couldn't stop my tone from changing. "And Zeke and Rochelle are still two peas in a pod."

He examined my face with his typical dark gaze, his shoulders looking powerful in his collared shirt. He was just as strong as he used to be. Experiencing grief hadn't physically changed him at all. His five o'clock shadow was thick like he skipped his shave that morning. "I detect some resentment there. You don't like Rochelle anymore?"

I didn't even talk to Ryker, and he picked up on my misery. I had to do a better job of hiding my feelings. "No, she's great. They're really cute together. He's so happy, and it's nice to see him like that."

Ryker still didn't buy it. "Are you sure?"

"Yeah..."

Ryker watched me like he didn't believe me, but he didn't press me on it. "So, there's something I want to ask, but I don't want to ask it." He stared at me like he'd given me enough information that I should be able to figure out what he wanted.

Sadly, I knew exactly what that question was. "No." I didn't want him to answer in return so I never asked. It didn't matter to me. Even if he was married, it wouldn't matter to me. He cut me deeper than a butcher's knife. I bled out and took months to put myself back together. That kind of heartache nearly killed me. I got back on my feet and moved on— thankfully. But that didn't mean I wanted to talk about it.

"I'm surprised."

"I don't know what that's supposed to mean."

"I figured someone would have swooped you up the second you were available." He gave me that knowing look, full of accusation. He brought his glass to his lips and took a deep drink.

"Zeke is happy with Rochelle."

"Not that happy. I saw the way he looked at you...he never looks at her like that."

The hope grew in my heart, inflating like a balloon. "Well, I'm pretty sure he's over me."

Ryker immediately tensed at what I said. "So you finally believe me?"

"Yes." I'd rather not admit Ryker was right about anything, but I wasn't going to lie just to keep my pride.

"He got the courage to tell you?" He gave me that dark smile, a fake and insincere one.

"No. Rochelle told me. I was surprised."

"Why did she tell you that?"

I didn't want to go into the details. "You know, girl talk."

"And?"

"And what?"

"That was it? Nothing happened?"

"Why would anything happen? Like I said, he's seeing Rochelle, and he's over me."

"I guess you must be right. Probably would have done something by now."

The hope disappeared like my balloon had been popped. I analyzed the words Zeke said to me on the phone the other day. When he said he missed me, I pretended it was in a completely different context. "Zeke is like family to me. And this way, he'll always be family. And Rochelle will just be a part of that."

"True."

I finished my wine but didn't order another. I didn't mind talking to Ryker, but I didn't want this to last longer than an hour. Maybe one day we could be around each other longer than that, but for now, we weren't quite there. "How's your mom?" I never met her. Actually, I'd only seen her once—at the funeral.

He stared down into his glass. "She's...having a hard time."

"I'm so sorry." If I lost my husband, I would be devastated too.

"Con and I spend a lot of time with her, keeping her company. But we'll never be able to replace what she lost."

It was the first time he talked about his brother. "That's nice of you. I'm sure she appreciates it."

"She's pretty quiet. We mainly watch TV with her. She used to never shut up, and now I can't even get her to answer a damn question." He chuckled slightly, but it was purely in a sarcastic way.

"Your dad was a good man. I still think about him."

"I know he was...and thank you."

Ironically, it was the deepest conversation we ever had—and we weren't even together anymore.

He opened his mouth like he was going to say something, but then he closed it again.

I remained patient, hoping for something more.

"I want you to know that...I really cared about you. I know I didn't show it very well and I hurt you, but I hope you can believe me."

I didn't want to talk about our relationship. I was hoping he'd say something about his father instead, get his grief off his chest. So I steered the conversation back in the right direction. "I know you did, Ryker. And it's okay we didn't work out. There's no need to apologize. I'm in a really good place in my life. I'm not sad we broke up. I'm glad it happened."

He watched me with his expressionless eyes, trying to read into mine.

"When my mother died, it was really hard for me to accept. I did a lot of stupid things. I got drunk at school and got suspended. I fooled around with boys when I was way too young for those kind of relationships. And I lost myself…"

His eyes softened.

"It's not just the ache of losing a parent. It's the fact that you feel alone. There's one less person you can rely on. And you think about them suffering…so you suffer too. But when Rex finally made me talk to him…really talk to him…it truly helped. I'm not suggesting that you talk to me about everything, but having that conversation with someone would be helpful."

He nodded with his eyes downcast.

I opened my wallet and left cash for my drink.

He didn't offer to pay, which I was grateful for.

"I should get going. It was nice to see you, Ryker." I got off the chair and pushed it under the table.

He didn't get up. "Did you like my flowers?"

I shouldered my purse and stared at him blankly, unsure what he meant. "I'm sorry."

"The flowers I sent you on your birthday. Just wanted to know if you liked them."

I still didn't have a clue what he was talking about. "Sorry...I never got them." Maybe the delivery guy didn't make it down to the lab. He probably left it on someone's desk and it just never made its way down to me.

He crossed his arms over his chest and didn't say anything. With his empty glass sitting in front of him, he looked completely lost. He had nowhere to go, no one to go home to. His eyes weren't as bright and vibrant as they once were. Like a cloud permanently obscuring the sun, his vision was masked.

Defeat and depression hung from his limbs, and he was no longer the charismatic and cocky man who could make my knees grow weak. Now he was tired, exhausted from the loss of his father. The burden of the dead still weighed heavily on his shoulders. He didn't look at me for nearly a minute, refusing to make eye contact with me, which wasn't like him at all. "You were right, Rae."

"Right about what?"

He clenched his jaw then looked out the window, seeing the spots of rain on the glass. "Right about everything."

Chapter Nine

Rex

I entered the bar with Tobias and shook off the rain from my jacket. "I've never been here before."

"Me neither. But I hear they have the best happy hour. Buy one app, get one free."

"Now that's a deal I can get on board with." I high-fived him for no real reason.

We walked to a table and took our seats. The menus were in front of us, so we took a quick glance over them.

"You're awfully cheap for a man who owns a successful bowling alley." With broad shoulders and hair as dark as mine, Tobias fit in right alongside Zeke and me.

"Well, I've got to pinch every penny so I can pay back Zeke and Rae."

"Are they acting like a bank?"

"No. They just—" I stopped talking when I spotted someone strangely familiar across the room.

With dark brown hair, a slender physique, and wearing jeans and a pink sweater with the hole at the bottom, was Rae. At least, I thought it was.

"What?" Tobias looked over his shoulder and followed my gaze. "Beautiful babe?"

"No...but I'm definitely looking at a pig."

"Hey. Isn't that...?"

I stared at Rae's profile but couldn't take it in. It really was her sitting across the room. She had a glass of wine in her hand, and the man who sat across from her was someone I absolutely despised. "What the fuck is she doing with Ryker?"

"Isn't she supposed to be in New York?"

What the hell was going on?

Just when I was about to confront her, she stood up and grabbed her purse. She left a ten on the table and prepared to leave.

"Keep your head down," I ordered. "I don't want her to see us."

Tobias buried his nose in the menu.

Rae exchanged a few more words with Ryker, but it was obvious they weren't pleasant ones. Ryker looked out the window and avoided her gaze. He wasn't his typical playful self. He looked pale and devastated, like there wasn't anything left for him to live for. Rae didn't give him a hug or even a handshake. She walked out without looking back.

Ryker remained behind, his eyes watching her walk away until she was completely out of sight.

I still couldn't figure out what I was looking at.

"What the hell is going on?" Tobias whispered. "Are you sure she didn't return from New York today?"

"No. She's supposed to be there for three more days."

"I wonder if she ever went at all…"

Now I wondered the same thing.

***

I called Kayden for answers. I wanted to get to the bottom of this, but I also wanted an excuse to talk to her. When I brought her soup, we didn't say much.

The phone rang a few times before it went to voicemail.

"Hey, it's Rex. Just calling to check in and see how you're doing. Haven't seen in you in a while..." My voice echoed over the line, and I suddenly felt incredibly lonely. I didn't bother mentioning what I saw with Rae. It didn't seem important anymore now that I was talking to her answering machine.

I called Jessie next.

She answered. "Hey, Rex. What's up?"

"I have a bone to pick with you."

"I'm not giving you free haircuts anymore. Look, you make money now, and I should be paid for my work."

"No, not about that. But, we'll get back to that because I actually do need a haircut."

"Not a free one," she countered.

"Whatever. I'm pissed right now, and you're going to give me some answers."

"Pissed?" she asked. "About what?"

"What the hell is going on with Rae?"

Silence. Long silence. Her tone changed from confrontational to bewildered. "What are you talking about?"

"Rae's not in New York. I just saw her having a drink with Ryker in some bar."

"What?" Now she sounded as shocked as I was. "With Ryker? Are you sure?"

"Yes. I stared at them for fifteen minutes."

"Oh god..."

"Jess, why did she lie?"

"I don't know why you think I know anything—"

"Because you do," I snapped. "I can tell. Why would she lie about going to New York but stay in Seattle? I know my sister does stupid shit, but I really can't figure this one out."

Jessie remained quiet, unsure what to say. "Look...I don't know."

"Bullshit. Tell me."

"Rex, I can't."

"You can't?" I asked incredulously. "No, you're gonna tell me."

"I promised her I wouldn't."

I met a dead end, and I didn't like it. "Why would she make you promise something like that?"

"Rex...I swore I wouldn't say anything. And I can't. I know you must feel really confused right now, and I feel bad about that. But I promise this whole thing has nothing to do with you."

"She's not trying to get away from me?"

"No."

"Is she back together with Ryker?" That was the worst scenario.

"No."

"Are you just saying that?"

"No," she said. "I have no idea why she was with Ryker, but her hiatus has nothing to do with him either."

"Then who does it have to do with?"

She sighed into the phone, and that was the only answer I was going to get.

"Don't tell her I'm on her trail."

"Rex, the second we get off the phone, I'm giving her a heads-up."

"No. She promised she wouldn't lie to me again." I couldn't stop the hurt from escaping my voice. "I'm going to give her some space to come clean to me when she supposedly comes back."

"Rex...if you knew why she lied, you wouldn't be angry with her."

My thoughts turned bleak. "Please don't tell me she's sick...not anything like that."

"No. I promise. Nothing like that."

I felt better, but now I couldn't think of any justifiable reason for her behavior.

"I understand why you're mad, Rex. But if you knew what was going on, I promise you wouldn't be mad."

"Yeah...but I don't know what's going on."

"I'm sure the shit will hit the fan soon."

"So, are you not going to tell her I know?" Jessie was very devoted to Rae, so the odds of getting what I wanted weren't good.

"I don't know…"

"Don't tell her, Jess."

She sighed into the phone again.

"I thought I was your friend too."

"Of course."

"Okay, you kept a promise to her about this little hiatus she made. And now you're going to make a promise to me that you won't tell her I spotted her."

After contemplating what I said, she finally agreed. "Fine."

"Thank you."

"Just remember…she's going through a hard time. Don't be a jerk."

Rather than being angrier, I was hurt Rae didn't tell me whatever was going on in her life. We were roommates, and we were family. But I didn't tell her everything either. Obviously, I never told her about Kayden. But I never snuck off for two weeks and lied about it. "We'll see."

***

Rae walked inside with her fake luggage and smothered Safari with kisses. "I missed you so much, boy." Safari licked her entire face, swiping his tongue along the side of her nose and even in her ear. "Wow, what a great kiss." She hugged him before she stood up again.

I stared her down and forced myself not to explode right then and there. "How was New York?"

"It was great. Had a lot of fun."

How could she lie so easily? Was she a psychopath? "Good..."

"But I'm glad to be home. Living in a hotel got old."

"Yeah...I'm sure." Especially a hotel just a few blocks away.

"How was your vacation from me?"

"It was okay. I spent all day cleaning the house yesterday to hide the horror I caused."

"Well, at least I don't have to look at it." She pulled her luggage into the bedroom. "I'm going to shower and do some laundry. Can you order a pizza?"

I watched her walk away, feeling my face turn bright red in anger. Like nothing happened, she pretended everything was perfectly normal. How did she do that? The only thing stopping me from screaming was the fact Jessie told me Rae did this for a specific reason and that she was going through a hard time. And more importantly, I would feel bad for giving her a hard time.

That was the only thing that held me back.

***

Jessie came over while Rae was still getting dressed. She looked at me and saw the anger still burning in my eyes. It'd been there since Rae came home yesterday. "You look...pissed."

"Because I am."

"I'm guessing you haven't said anything to her."

"No." But it was getting more difficult with every passing hour.

"I'm proud of you. But I also think you should let it go."

Like I'd ever let this go. It was an insult she couldn't be honest with me—her family.

"I think—" She stopped talking when Rae came back into the room. She quickly changed the subject so it wasn't obvious we were just talking about her. "I think we need to pull Kayden out of her cave. She's been sick forever. There's no way she's still sick."

"I agree," Rae said. "We'll stop by her place and drag her with us."

My mood picked up slightly. The thought of seeing Kayden again brought a slight joy to my step. I hadn't seen her at all since I ended our arrangement. I found myself thinking about her all the time, wondering if she needed anything while she was ill. I brought her soup so I could spend time with her, but she wouldn't even let me inside.

"Sounds like a plan," Jessie said. "And you look hot, by the way."

"You look hotter," Rae replied.

I cleared my throat. "Eh-hem." I brushed the invisible dust from my shoulder.

"What?" Rae stared at me blankly.

"I look hot too, right?" I gave them my signature smolder.

"You want your sister to call you hot?" Rae asked incredulously.

"No, idiot," I snapped. "Jessie."

"Just tell him he's hot so we can get going," Rae said. "Otherwise, he'll bitch and complain the whole time."

"I don't bitch and complain," I said. "That's all you."

Jessie looked me up and down. "I think you look hot, Rex."

My ego hung on to her words even though I knew she didn't mean a word she said. "Why, thank you very much."

"Can we go now?" Rae walked out the door with Jessie, not bothering to wait for me.

"Shut up. I'm coming."

***

"Open this damn door!" Jessie nearly broke it down with her fists. "We know you're in there, brat!"

"She's really going to want to come out now…" Rae's voice was full of sarcasm.

"I don't care," Jessie said. "She doesn't even know you were in New York for ten days. That means we seriously need to talk."

My anger started to bubble again.

Rae gave it a try. "Kay, it's us. How sick can you be to not open the door?"

Finally, Kayden snapped the door open. She was in baggy sweats and a t-shirt. Her hair was thrown into a bun, and her face was free of makeup. She looked much skinnier than the last time I saw her—dangerously skinny. She opened her to mouth to say something, and then her eyes landed on mine. A short burst of panic overtook her face. Then she quickly hid it. "You almost broke down my door."

"I would have if Rae hadn't stopped me," Jessie said. "Are you still sick or what?"

"You don't look sick," Rae said. "Just tired."

Kayden closed the door more so we could see less of her. "I feel a lot better now. It was really nasty for a while there. I've just been taking the last few days easy so I can fully recover."

"What did you have?" Jessie asked.

"The flu," Kayden answered. "And then I got bronchitis."

"Damn," Rae said. "No wonder you were off the map."

"Yeah…" Kayden continued to eye us on her doorstep. "I would let you in, but I haven't scrubbed down the place since I've gotten better. I don't want you guys to get sick."

"That's okay," Rae said. "We actually wanted to pick you up. We're going to the bars and you're coming along."

"Yep," Jessie said. "Get dressed."

I hadn't said a word. When I looked at her, I froze.

"Uh…" Kayden turned around to look at something behind her.

"You're coming with us," Jessie demanded. "So don't fight it."

"Well, do you guys mind if I change real quick?" Kayden turned back to us.

"Not at all," Rae said.

"That's the spirit," Jessie said. "We'll wait out here."

"Alright," Kayden said. "I'll be back in fifteen minutes."

***

Like she just stepped out of the salon, Kayden looked like a beauty queen. With beautiful and shiny hair and a tight little dress that showed off her incredible legs, she looked like Miss Universe.

I couldn't stop staring.

After we arrived at the bar, we got our drinks and entered a booth in the corner. I sat right across from Kayden and had to force myself to gaze around the room so I wouldn't stare at her.

"Where's Zeke?" Jessie asked.

"He'll be here soon," I said. "Rochelle got off work late."

Jessie immediately turned her gaze to Rae.

Rae met the look then quickly turned away.

What was that about?

Kayden sipped her drink and didn't make eye contact with me once. She was silent at the table, searching the crowd and not participating in the conversation at all.

"You've lost a lot of weight," Jessie said. "You need to eat it back pronto."

"Or it's the best diet ever," Rae said with a laugh.

"Yeah, I know," Kayden said with a weak voice. "Every time I would eat something, I'd just throw up."

Jessie cringed. "That sucks. Sorry, girl."

"It's okay," Kayden said. "It's over now."

Jessie's focus turned to a guy at the bar. "Ooh...he's hunky."

Kayden followed her gaze. "Yeah, he is."

"I'm thinking about going for it," Jessie said. "But I'm kinda boxed in."

"Well, I'm gonna get up." Kayden pushed her drink away. "But only because I'm going to hit on him." Without another word, she left the booth and walked to the man sitting at the bar. She gave him a friendly smile, opened with some kind of joke, and then she was sitting beside him in the chair and making small talk.

Ouch.

Fuck, that hurt.

"Damn," Jessie said. "Did you see that?"

"I know," Rae said. "Being locked up for nearly three weeks probably made her go a little crazy. The ultimate dry spell."

"I would be jealous," Jessie said. "But I'm too impressed to feel anything less than admiration."

"Come to think of it, I don't think I've ever seen Kayden hit on a guy like that." Rae stirred her cocktail before she took a drink.

"I guess she really wants that D," Jessie said. "Good for her."

I kept staring at Kayden as she flirted with the handsome stranger. She said something to make him laugh, and then he ordered a round of drinks for both of them.

My stomach bubbled with acid.

I felt sick.

Like, worse than the flu and bronchitis sick.

"You alright, Rex?" Jessie asked.

I turned back to them and tried to mask my depression. "Yeah, this beer isn't for me. Too sweet." I made a face and pushed it away. Truthfully, it was perfectly fine.

"I hate it when that happens," Rae said. "A waste of eight bucks."

"Yeah…" I refused to let myself look at Kayden again. It just bummed me out.

"Zeke is here." Jessie spotted him enter the bar. "And she's with him…"

Rae purposely looked down at her drink and downed nearly half of it.

Zeke and Rochelle got a drink from the bar then joined us in the booth. "Hey, what's crackin'?" Zeke slid in first, and then Rochelle sat down right after him. Rae had to scoot next to me, followed by Jessie.

"Nothing much," I said. "Just hanging…"

Rochelle said hi to everyone. "Hey, guys." Then she focused her attention on Rae. "How was New York?"

Rae was quiet for so long it seemed like she didn't hear the question. She gripped her glass tightly and opened her mouth to speak, but nothing came out.

I eyed her with interest, unable to recall a time when my sister was speechless.

"It was good," Rae finally said. "But I'm glad to be home." She never made eye contact with Rochelle. She didn't look at Zeke either.

Jessie stared at her with a look full of pure sadness. Then she cleared her throat. "Kayden is here." She pointed across the bar. "Picking up some man candy."

"Oh, she is?" Zeke asked with genuine excitement. "I haven't seen her in weeks."

"Me neither," Rochelle said.

"Good for her," Zeke said. "That must have been a really nasty cold." He turned back to Rae. "When did you get back?"

Rae seemed revolted by the attention he was giving her. If I didn't know how close they were, I would think she hated him. They'd been in the same room together since I told her how he used to feel and she didn't behave differently then, so I knew that had nothing to do with this. "Yesterday."

"Was the house in disarray?" Zeke teased.

Rae didn't get the joke at all. "Uh, no."

Zeke's eyebrows rose. "Everything okay, Rae?"

"Yeah." Her voice cracked when she spoke. "I think I'm coming down with whatever Kayden had..." She touched her throat like she was looking for swelling.

"I can check your lymph nodes..." Zeke reached across the table.

Rae practically slapped his hand away. "Don't touch me."

Everyone at the table stilled at the harshness in her voice.

Jessie was the only one who didn't seem surprised. "So I cut this kid's hair yesterday and nearly cut off his ear."

We launched into a conversation about that, taking the attention off Rae. But I certainly didn't stop thinking about it. Jessie told us about her restless client and then talked about this hot guy she had right after him. Rochelle cozied up to Zeke and pressed her face right against his neck, cuddling with him like they were at home. Zeke turned to her, smiled, and then gave her a small kiss on the lips.

That's when Rae nearly pushed me. "Get up, Rex. I need to go to the bathroom." She bossed me around a lot, but the tone in her voice was different this time. I immediately obeyed because it felt like life or death.

Rae stormed off like she couldn't get away fast enough.

Jessie watched her walk off then continued sharing her adventures at work even though her story wasn't really that interesting. It seemed like she was telling it just for the sake of talking.

I sat down and tried to think of what could be bothering Rae—because something clearly was.

"Rex, what's up with Rae?" Zeke asked me point blank. "Seems like something is really bothering her. Did something happen in New York?"

"Not that I know of. But then again, she doesn't tell me jack shit." My anger seeped out like hot wax.

Zeke clearly picked up on the tension but didn't ask about it.

Rochelle spoke next. "Maybe someone should check on her—"

"I'll do it." Jessie immediately slid to my side of the booth so she could get out.

My patience was waning, and now I really wanted to get to the bottom of this. My sister lied to me about where she was for ten days, and now she was acting strange all over again. What was the big deal? Was she pregnant? Did Dad contact her? What could it possibly be that she wouldn't tell me? "No. I'm gonna check on her."

"I got it," Jessie said quickly. "I'm her best friend—"

"And I'm her brother." I slid out of the booth and marched to the bathroom, doing my best to ignore Kayden flirting with the guy at the bar. She was back on her feet and ready to mingle, and I hadn't even asked a woman out yet.

I walked to the hallway where the bathrooms were, and fortunately, there wasn't a line. I opened the door to the girl's bathroom because I knew that's where she would be. As I expected, Rae was standing in front of the mirror. She gripped either side of the sink and stared at the drain.

And she was crying.

She wasn't sobbing. Only a few tears leaked from the corner of her eyes and dripped down her face. She concentrated on her breathing and kept herself calm. She was a bomb about to explode, and she was doing everything she could to remain steady. When she heard the door shut, she looked at my reflection in the mirror.

And her look changed to panic. "What the hell are you doing in here?"

Whatever rage I had was gone when I saw Rae cry. I'd hardly ever seen her shed a tear. Instead of giving in to her pain, she held her head high and remained strong. Whatever made her break down like this was huge. It had to be. "I wanted to see if you were okay..."

"I'm fine." She snatched a paper towel from the dispenser and quickly dabbed the water that seeped under her eyes. "I have really bad allergies this time of year."

It was bullshit and I knew it. She knew it too.

I came closer to her then leaned against the wall. I crossed my arms over my chest and stared at her, not caring we were standing in the middle of the women's restroom. Thankfully, no one else was inside. "Rae, what the hell is going on? First, you lie to me about being in New York for ten days, and now you're an emotional wreck."

Her eyes snapped open, and the look she gave me was full of utter fear. "What?"

"Yes, I know you weren't really in New York. You lied to me—again. But I'm prepared to let that go if you give me a damn good reason why."

It was clear I knew the truth so she didn't try to lie her way out of it. "How did you know?"

"I went out with Tobias and saw you with Ryker."

Her face turned pale.

"Please tell me you aren't with him again."

She stared at the drain again. "No."

"Then what was that about?"

She sighed and closed her eyes for a moment, gathering her answer. "He realized I was staying at the hotel across the street from COLLECT. So he followed me and asked me why I was living out of a suitcase. We got a drink and talked about it. That was it."

At least she wasn't seeing him again. That was something to be grateful for. "Why were you staying at a hotel to begin with?"

She closed her eyes like she didn't want to answer me.

"Rae, you're going to give me a sufficient answer. Otherwise, I'm going to make your life a living hell."

She still wouldn't answer me. "Rex, I understand you're mad. But I'm not ready to talk about why I lied about New York. Please...just be patient with me."

"No." I'd never been a patient man. "And why are you crying right now? Why did you storm off into the bathroom? What did anyone say that would bother you so much—" I stopped in midsentence when the answer dawned on me. Right before Rae got up, Zeke kissed Rochelle. And before that, Rae and Jessie were being weird about Rochelle. Did I just figure it out? "Zeke."

She straightened and let go of the sink.

"Holy fucking shit! You like Zeke!" I gripped my scalp because I couldn't believe the truth I'd just uncovered. It was the only thing that made sense, as crazy as it sounded.

And she didn't deny it. "Keep your voice down."

"How?" I demanded. "When did this start?"

"I don't know...a few weeks ago."

My heart was beating harder than horse hooves against the earth. "I can't believe this...but it doesn't explain why you lied about New York."

She dabbed her eyes again until they were dry. Then she tossed the towel in the trash. "Look, I just needed some space. Since you live with me, he always comes by. I needed some time to stop thinking about him. I wasn't going to achieve that if he was always sitting on my couch. So...I tried to get away."

"Why are you trying to get over him?"

"Because of Rochelle, you idiot."

I ignored the unfair insult because she was just upset.

"She's a really nice person, and Zeke is crazy about her. You think I don't feel like shit for looking at him like this? He has a girlfriend. I shouldn't be feeling this way. It's wrong on so many levels. I refuse to be that kind of person. He belongs to Rochelle, and I'm a bitch for dreaming about him, for thinking about him all the time..."

"You dream about him?"

She didn't elaborate on that part.

And I suspected why. A moment of awkwardness passed between us.

"I thought it was just a physical crush, and if I didn't see him for a while, I would stop thinking about him."

"And I guess that didn't work?"

"No. Seeing him kiss Rochelle right now just made me...feel terrible."

I never thought Rae would have feelings for Zeke, but here she was confessing her broken heart over a man she couldn't have. "This is unbelievable. Did you feel this way after I told you how he used to feel?"

"No. I felt this way before. I'm not exactly sure why or when...but when you told me how he used to feel, it just made everything worse."

This was juicy enough to be a soap opera. "So...are you in love with him?"

"I don't know... That's a strong thing to say. But these feelings are undeniable. And they're killing me."

If Zeke knew this, he would pass out. "You should tell him."

She immediately turned vicious. "Don't be ridiculous."

"I'm serious, Rae. After the way he felt about you, he'd be over the moon about this." He told me word-for-word he could see himself settling down with Rae. That wasn't something you just said to anybody.

"Aren't you forgetting someone?" She turned her hateful look on me. "Rochelle? The woman he loves?"

"Yeah, but—"

"But nothing. He's moved on with someone else. And Rochelle is great. I missed my chance when I dated Ryker. That's the end of the story."

"Rochelle has nothing on you, Rae."

"What's that supposed to mean?"

"I know he felt differently with you than he does with her."

Rae shook her head. "You can't make an assumption like that. And even if you're right, it doesn't matter. That was in the past. Now we're in the present, and in the present, he's been dating Rochelle for six months."

"He could date her for a lifetime and still not feel what he did with you."

Her eyes softened for just an instant before they hardened again. "Rex, it doesn't matter. I'm not telling him."

"But—"

"I love him and would never do that to him. Do you have any idea what kind of position that would put him in? It would just confuse him. And if it didn't confuse him because he's in love with Rochelle, which he is, it would just strain our relationship. Rochelle wouldn't like me anymore, not that I could blame her, and she wouldn't want Zeke to be around me at all. It's got disaster written all over it."

She made up her mind and clearly wasn't going to change it. And I wasn't going to tell her about Zeke's upcoming proposal. That would just make her feel worse. "Then what's the alternative?"

"I'll get over him." She looked in the mirror like she was trying to convince herself of what she just said. "I'll start dating again and try to find a good guy. Maybe I'll find someone so great I'll forget about Zeke altogether."

I already knew that plan wouldn't work. "I really think you should tell him."

"Well, I don't agree."

"Let me ask you this." I leaned against the wall again and watched her. "When you were starting to see Ryker, would you rather have known Zeke had feelings for you? Do you wish he would have told you?"

She looked into my eyes, the look expressionless.

"Do you?" I pressed.

"I don't know…"

"Ryker ended up being a big, fat mistake. Maybe Zeke would have saved you time."

"Rochelle isn't an asshole like Ryker is. And I had no idea what was going to happen with Ryker. There's no way to predict what I would have done."

"But you might have done something differently if you had all the facts up front."

"Maybe...but I didn't have feelings for him back then."

"But if you'd known how he felt, you might have."

She leaned against the opposite wall and crossed her arms over her chest. "We can play what-if all day long, but that's not going to change anything. I'm not telling him, Rex. Rochelle is wonderful. I couldn't call myself a friend if I did anything to jeopardize their relationship."

If this were any other situation, I'd probably agree with her. But it wasn't. Zeke and Rae were two people who were so much alike, it was freaky. Even I could picture them spending the rest of their lives together, being happy and nerdy every single day. And I definitely wasn't the romantic type.

"You better not tell Zeke any of this."

I held her gaze.

"I mean it, Rex. It's not your place."

All I could think about was how quickly Zeke rushed into this thing with Rochelle. He even admitted he didn't start dating her for the right reasons. And I suspected he didn't want to marry her for the right reasons either. Something felt off with her from the beginning. "Okay."

"Thank you." Rae leaned her head against the wall and looked up at the fluorescent lights. "I don't want to go back out there. I don't want to sit there and pretend I'm having a good time while he sticks his tongue down her throat."

I didn't want to go out there either. Kayden would still be hitting on that guy, and they'd have a few laughs as they downed their drinks. Or maybe they wouldn't even be out there anymore. Maybe he already took her home.

What a shitty night.

***

I couldn't decide what to do.

A part of me wanted to spill the beans to Zeke. He should know that he had a chance with Rae if he still wanted it. And it didn't seem like Rae just liked him. It was a lot more than that. Strong enough to make her live in a hotel for ten days so she wouldn't think about him.

But I also felt like a dick for saying anything. Rae asked me to keep it to myself, and Rochelle was the one about to get screwed over. She was a nice person who didn't deserve to get her heart broken. But at the same time, that was just how life was. Sometimes you got hurt.

And then I might ruin something great for Zeke. His relationship with Rochelle would probably work out. He already bought the ring, asked her father for permission, and planned his proposal. If I told him the truth, it would just screw everything up.

And he and Rae might not last forever. It could be a short-term thing before they realized they were better off as friends.

Zeke might lose someone he was perfectly happy with.

I couldn't decide.

Every time I made one decision, I switched back over. And just when I finalized my plans, a new thought popped into my mind to make me change direction.

I wished someone would just tell me what to do.

Rae parked her rear on the couch for the next week. She went to work, came home, and did absolutely nothing. She didn't jog through the park with Safari or even take care of the apartment. She left her dirty dishes in the sink and only did laundry when she ran out of clothes to wear.

It was weird.

I didn't like this side of Rae. This dirty and messy one. Now I understood why living with me was so insufferable.

"You doing okay?" I finally got to the point where I needed to ask her. She probably wanted the space, but since I lived there, it was impossible to give it to her.

"I'm fine." She pulled a blanket over her lap and read on her Kindle.

"You don't seem fine."

"I've just been tired lately…"

"Well, there're no groceries in the fridge, no clean dishes in the cabinets, and this place hasn't been vacuumed in over a week."

She didn't have the energy to be a smartass. "Whatever."

Damn, this was worse than I thought. "What was it like talking to Ryker?"

She shrugged. "He's pretty depressed over his father. His playful personality is completely gone. I feel terrible for him…"

"Yeah, I do too." I would always hate him for what he did to Rae, but I did pity him for losing a parent. When Rae and I lost our mom, we were devastated. And then our father left a long time ago, so his absence felt even more real.

"But in time, he'll get better. We all fall down. It takes some time to get back up."

"Yeah…"

Her hair was in a messy bun, and she wore the same pajamas she'd been wearing all week. Whenever Zeke wanted to hang out, I made sure we did stuff outside the apartment so she wouldn't have to see him. But in the back of my mind, I couldn't stop picturing a reality where they were dating. Zeke would be here all the time, and they would both be with people who were good enough for each other. They

233

would be happy, and I wouldn't have to see Rae depressed on the couch every single day.

But if I told Zeke the truth, would he pick Rochelle?

Or would he pick Rae?

***

"Everything alright?" Zeke sat across from me and dug into his hot wings. We just finished a game of basketball, which I lost horribly.

My mind wasn't in the game. I kept thinking about the critical information that I held. Would I be a bad friend if I didn't tell him? Or would I be a bad friend if I did tell him? Either way, I lost. "Just got a lot on my mind."

"Like what?"

"Just work and stuff..."

"Is Rae doing better? She was really weird at the bar last week."

"Yeah...it's that time of the month."

Zeke took my word for it and returned to eating his hot wings. His eyes moved to the TV screen in the corner.

"So…plans are still underway to propose?"

"Yeah. I can't believe I'll be engaged in a week. Pretty crazy, huh?"

"Yeah…" Zeke seemed happy when I asked him so it was probably best if I didn't tell him. But if I changed my mind later, it would be worse. If I told him while he was engaged to Rochelle, then I really would be a bad friend. "It is crazy." Especially since he'd only been seeing this woman for like six months.

Zeke detected my tone again. "I hate asking more than once, but it seems like something is up. You've been a grouch all week."

"I'm not a grouch," I snapped. I'd just had a lot on my mind. I kept wondering if Kayden went home with that guy. On top of that, I had this stupid romance situation with my sister to worry about. If I didn't do something about it, nothing would ever happen.

"You're definitely a grouch. You've been weird, Rae has been weird, Jessie has been weird…even Kayden has been weird. I get the impression you all know something I don't."

Maybe he was more observant than I gave him credit for.

"Are you going to leave me hanging or what?"

I thought it was ironic that we were going to have this conversation now, at the same joint where he told me he was going to ask Rae out. Actually, we were at the same table too, to top it off. "Alright, something is up…"

Zeke wiped the sauce off his fingers and gave me his full attention.

"It's a big deal, and I don't even know where to begin. I've debated telling you this all week. Either way, I'm a bad friend."

"What do you mean?"

"I'm a jackass for telling you this. But I'm also a jackass if I don't."

"Wow...this should be interesting." He rested his elbows on the table. "Lay it on me."

"Okay..." Here goes nothing. "When Rae stormed off last week, I followed her into the bathroom to check on her. And that's when she told me what's been up with her lately."

Zeke didn't blink as he stared me down.

"Basically, she told me she has feelings for you. She didn't actually go to New York. She stayed at a hotel near work just so she could have a break from you, to see if she could get over you. And when you and Rochelle were being lovey-dovey at the bar, she went into the bathroom and shed a few tears..."

Zeke didn't react at all. Still as a statue, he took in the words without really processing them. He seemed to be in shock. After nearly a minute of silence, his lips finally moved. "I... What... I don't understand." His face finally slackened as all the emotions hit him at once. "Rae has feelings for me?"

I nodded.

"Me?" He pointed at his chest.

I nodded again.

His eyes widened incredulously. "She said those words?"

"Yes. She said she's been dreaming about you and can't stop thinking about you."

"I..." He fell speechless all over again and leaned back in the chair. He ran his fingers through his hair, shocked. "When?"

I knew what he was really asking. "A few weeks ago. She says she doesn't remember exactly when her feelings started. And then...Rochelle told her you used to have feelings for her."

"She did what?" he snapped.

"And when Rae heard that...her feelings intensified. Now it's hard for her to be around you guys...for obvious reasons. She feels guilty because you're seeing Rochelle and she has no right to feel this way. She really likes Rochelle and wants things to work out between you."

"She knows how I feel about her?"

I couldn't ignore the tense he used. "Yeah. She came to me asking questions, and I basically told her everything." I knew he wouldn't get mad at me. I only did it because Rochelle spilled the beans first.

"I can't believe this…" He ran his fingers through his hair again, unable to sit still for even a few seconds.

"I can't believe it either."

"Why didn't she tell me herself? Rae isn't shy."

"Because you're seeing Rochelle. She never wants to come between you two. She respects Rochelle."

"So she has no idea you're telling me this?"

I shook my head. "I wasn't going to tell you because you're proposing to Rochelle next week. But…I also thought it would be a mistake if I didn't tell you. I know how you used to feel about Rae, and I thought you should have all the information up front before you do anything. I'm sorry if I've confused you or messed things up... I'm not good at this sort of thing."

"No. I'm glad you told me." He rested his elbows on the table again.

I waited for him to say something else, to tell me he'd made a decision about what to do.

But he remained quiet.

So I sat there awkwardly.

Zeke looked across the restaurant and ran his fingers through his hair again.

"What are you thinking?"

"I don't know..."

I sipped my beer and waited for him to form coherent thoughts.

"I've always wanted Rae. She's exactly what I want in a partner. I can't count the number of times I've been with her and I just wanted to grab her and kiss her."

I stopped myself from making a disgusted face.

"I've been into her for three years, on and off. When I pictured myself getting married, it was always to her. She's the most incredible woman I've ever met. She's gorgeous, smart, outgoing, humble and...goddamn perfect."

I drank my beer again just so I had something to do.

"But I have Rochelle now. And she's pretty, smart, outgoing, and has a lot of other great qualities. We have a lot in common because she's a doctor, and she comes from a family of doctors. She's sweet and never has a bad thing to say about anyone. I don't have a single complaint."

"That's rough..."

He sighed then covered his face. "But she's not Rae..."

Did that mean what I thought it meant?

"But I already bought the ring, planned the dinner, and talked to her parents..." He dragged his hand down his face and sighed again. "I pretty much already committed to her. I was planning on asking her to move in with me right away. Everything is planned and ready to go..."

I held my tongue and didn't say anything. I couldn't make this decision for him even though the answer was obvious. "What are you going to do then?"

"I don't fucking know, Rex."

Maybe I shouldn't have said anything. "I can only imagine how difficult this is for you. But at least you have two beautiful women who love you." I forced a chuckle but it died in my throat.

"Nothing is funny about this. Either way, I hurt someone."

"Rae doesn't count. She was the one who chose to have feelings for you while you had a girlfriend. So if you do stay with Rochelle, don't feel bad for Rae."

"I'll always feel bad anytime Rae is in pain."

Now the choice was even more obvious.

He rose from his chair. "I've got to go... I need some time to think."

"Okay. Good luck."

He threw some cash on the table with a defeated look in his eyes. "Thanks. I'm gonna need it."

Ray of Love

Chapter Ten

Rae

I wasn't eating enough and my jeans started to feel loose. I'd always wanted to lose a little extra weight, but I knew my current approach wasn't healthy because I simply wasn't eating. Every time I thought about Zeke kissing Rochelle, I wanted to throw up.

I was a horrible, horrible person.

On my lunch break, I decided to walk down the street and head to the café. Today, I was going to force myself to have a reasonable lunch. The lack of food slowed my metabolism way down, and I felt sluggish all the time. I didn't have enough stamina to carry out projects without feeling exhausted.

I stood in line and stared at the menu, trying to find something appetizing. My stomach didn't rumble like it usually did by ten in the morning, but I'd have to pick something—anything. The Kickin' Blue Chicken sounded pretty good. Maybe I'd get that.

"Hey." That beautiful and masculine voice came into my ear, sounding soothing like a waterfall. But it also brought me complete misery. My pulse picked up, and I suddenly felt weak.

I turned to face Zeke. He was wearing his blue scrubs, looking muscular and toned in the loose fabric. His blue eyes stood out against his clothing, and his cleanly shaven jaw looked nice. His mouth was kissable—like always. "Oh, hey…" I forced myself to sound enthused but it still only came out half-assed. The last thing I needed was to come face-to-face with the man I couldn't have.

He looked into my eyes without his usual friendliness. In fact, he seemed down. There wasn't a spring in his step or even the hint of an upcoming smile. "Hey." He repeated himself like he didn't greet me in the first place.

The line moved up so I took a step forward. "Getting lunch?" Our conversation didn't flow well like it used to. Now, it was just tense and awkward. But that had to just be my perception of what was happening. You know, because I was stupidly hung up on him.

"Yeah. The schedule cleared up so I get to eat again." He chuckled but it wasn't sincere whatsoever.

"Oh, yeah. Glad that worked out." I took another step forward when the line moved.

He stood beside me, keeping a few feet between us. "What are you getting?"

"Number twelve."

"I guess I'll get that too."

When we reached the register, we both ordered together. Zeke tried to pay, like always, but I threw my cash at the employee. Normally, Zeke would pull some stunt so I wouldn't have to pay for anything, but this time, he didn't fight it at all. It was almost like he wanted me to pay for myself.

We grabbed our food and sat together at a table.

"You know, if you need to get back to work, you don't need to eat with me..." I was looking for any excuse to get rid of him. How could I sit across from the man of my dreams and not stare at him with desperation? When I was this close to him, I pictured those arms wrapped tightly around me. And his lips were pressed against mine, soft and aggressive. I fantasized about those strong hands running through my hair and gripping me by the back of the neck. I imagined how his powerful chest would feel against mine when he was on top of me and thrusting into me, sweat dripping down his front just like it did when we played ball together. I pictured him making love to me and telling me he loved me—just like in my dreams.

"I want to eat with you."

His words snapped me out of my daydream. "Oh...cool."

The awkward silence descended again. Zeke kept looking at me during our meal, staring at me more often than he normally did. He ate his food at a much slower rate than usual. He seemed to be as uncomfortable around me as I was around him.

I ate half of my sandwich because that was all I could manage. I still had fifteen minutes before I had to head back to the lab, but I wanted to call it early. Being this close to him was torture, not pleasurable. "I should head back. I'll see you around."

"Yeah, I should get going too." He didn't get up from his seat.

I moved first and grabbed my tray. "Uh…see you later."

"Yeah. Have a good day." He stared at me hard, not blinking as he looked at me.

When the gaze became too much, I turned away. I tossed my garbage then piled the tray on top of the cabinet. I could feel his stare burn into my back the entire time. Even when I left the restaurant, I could still feel it. It wasn't until I was back in the lab that I finally felt free of his presence.

But even then, my heart would never feel free.

Ray of Love

Chapter Eleven

Rex

I need to talk to you.

I saw Zeke's message and immediately knew what it was about. *I'm home right now.*

Meet me at Mega Shake in fifteen minutes.

Okay. It wouldn't be a great idea to have this conversation while Rae was in her bedroom.

I left the apartment without saying goodbye to her and headed down to the burger joint. When I arrived, he was already there. He had our food placed in front of him on two trays since he knew exactly what I liked.

I sat across from him but didn't take a single fry. "What's up?"

Zeke looked empty and depressed, like he lost everything that mattered to him. I hadn't seen him this low since his nana died. "I broke up with Rochelle."

I tensed in my chair, feeling chills enter my body. "You did?"

He nodded. "It sucked, man. It was torture. She cried..."

I knew how much she loved Zeke just by watching them together. It didn't surprise me that was her reaction.

"She was devastated." He shook his head with self-loathing.

"What did you tell her?"

"I told her we had a great time together, but I just didn't feel the same way anymore...which is true. Since you told me about Rae, I haven't even been able to kiss Rochelle. I felt too guilty."

"Guilty in what way?"

"Guilty that I'm seriously debating between two different women," he said coldly, in regards to himself. "Rochelle doesn't deserve that. She's an amazing person."

I knew Rochelle was going to get hurt eventually. I'd foreseen it when Zeke moved their relationship at lightning speed. He was in a hurry to get to the finish line, and Rochelle went along with it.

"I could barely touch her hand. I couldn't even get hard."

"Stress does a lot to the body..."

"All I could think about was what it would be like to be with Rae. But then I realized I was wrong. I was with Rochelle first, and I was even happy with her. I could be happy with her for the rest of my life. So I decided to just forget Rae and stick with Rochelle. But then...I ran into Rae on my lunch break."

"Oh..."

"And we didn't say much to each other but...I could feel it."

"What?"

"I could feel the chemistry, the desperation. I could feel the need to be together. I could see the sadness in her eyes that she couldn't have me. And...I realized I needed to be with Rae. Even if it doesn't work out, I'll regret not knowing if I don't at least try.

Whatever Rae has...it's special. Rochelle is great and perfect but...she doesn't have whatever it is Rae has."

That's some deep shit.

"I feel like an asshole for what I've done to Rochelle. Even when I broke up with her, I knew I shouldn't do it. But I couldn't stop myself. The second you told me about Rae, my body came to life. I don't just want her. But I need her. It's always been her..."

"So...when are you going to talk to her?"

"Not for a while," he said quickly. "I just broke up with Rochelle, and I still love her. I need some time to get over our relationship before I can move on. I can't just jump into bed with Rae. As much as I want to, it wouldn't feel right. Besides, Rae deserves to be the only woman in my heart. And Rochelle deserves some respect. If she knew I slept with Rae the next day....it would kill her."

I nodded in agreement. "I see what you mean."

"So...I'm just gonna chill for a while."

When the dust settled and the two of them finally started their relationship, I knew things would get better. Right now, the two people closest to me were absolutely miserable. But in time, that would pass.

They just had to be patient.

Ray of Love

Chapter Twelve

Rae

"Look at all the phone numbers I got." Kayden sat down in the booth and counted out fifteen phone numbers written on napkins.

My eyes nearly popped out.

Jessie pressed her hand against her chest and gasped. "Shit, girl."

"You got all of those?" I held up the pile in my hand then sorted through them.

"Yep," Kayden said proudly.

"Tonight?" I asked incredulously.

"Yep," Kayden said again. "I have some sweet moves…"

"I don't know if I think you're awesome or just a slut," Jessie said.

"Oh, I'm totally a slut," Kayden said. "But an awesome one. I think I'm going to call up this guy first." She pointed at the napkin on top. "He's really fine."

I'd never seen Kayden hit on a guy, let alone land fifteen numbers. Jessie was the most outgoing of the three of us, and she never scored that many guys in a single night. "Well...good for you. Looks like you're recovering from that cold pretty well."

"I'm totally over that cold," she said with venom. "That cold is in the past, and I'm a new woman." She scanned the room and set her eyes on a new target. "Excuse me, I have a bull to ride." She flipped her hair over one shoulder and strutted to the guy she laid eyes on.

Jessie looked at me, still in shock. "Congrats to her but..." She couldn't finish her sentence because she didn't know what to say.

"It's not like her, huh?"

"Not at all. She went from seeing a guy maybe once every few months to seeing a new one every night."

"I know..."

"I don't know if we should be worried or not. I mean, she's a big girl who can take care of herself."

"You're right, she is. I just hope she's not jumping the gun and taking on more than she can handle." Maybe she had a sudden boost of self-confidence after she recovered from her illness. She probably had cabin fever from being cooped up for so long, and now she was ready to spring to life. "I'm sure it's fine and we're just overthinking it."

Jessie downed her drink then changed the subject. "So...Rex knows about Zeke?"

"I told him."

"And he took it well?"

"He was surprised but didn't say much else."

"He wouldn't tell Zeke, right?"

"No." I wasn't worried about that. He wouldn't be a good friend to Zeke if he did. "That wouldn't help anyone."

"Was he mad you lied about New York?"

"Not really. Once I explained why, I think he understood."

"He'd have to be heartless not to."

"Yeah. I saw Zeke the other day when I was on my lunchbreak… That was awkward."

"Why?" she asked.

"I just felt…different. It's probably just me but he wasn't very talkative either. It didn't feel the way it used to. I guess me having feelings for him has totally screwed me up in the head."

She nodded in agreement. "It makes you see things that aren't really there."

"Yeah, true."

"Well, I'm sure you'll get over him eventually. You just need to get under someone new."

***

"Heads-up. Zeke is coming over." Rex sat in front of the TV while he played his racing game on his PS4.

"Why don't you guys go out?"

He shrugged.

"Or go to his place?"

"Why don't you just grow up and stop avoiding him?" He made a sharp turn but spun out. "He's your friend and shouldn't be treated like a criminal."

"I'm not treating him like a criminal—"

"Then be his friend again, not this weird and awkward chick."

"Ugh." I grabbed a pillow from the couch and threw it at his head. "You're a pain in the ass sometimes."

"All the time," he said. "Don't sugarcoat it."

There was a knock on the door before Zeke walked inside. "It's me."

My hair was in a bun, and I wore leggings with a baggy sweater. If I'd known he was coming, I wouldn't have dressed like a mess. "Hey. Rex is being a pain in the ass, like always."

Zeke set a case of beer on the counter before he walked into the living room. "I guess I can't say I'm

261

surprised." He stood on the opposite side of the couch and looked at me, his blue eyes full of something that couldn't be described.

I stared back and suddenly felt weightless, like he was sucking me deep into his eyes.

Rex must have picked up on it because he suddenly cleared his throat. "I tried to break my record but Rae made me crash. She screwed the whole thing up."

Zeke's eyes never left my face. "That sucks, man. I'm glad I don't live with my sister."

"I wouldn't mind living with your sister." He waggled his eyebrows.

Zeke finally broke eye contact with me. "You want to die, man?"

"Come on," Rex said. "We'd have beautiful babies together."

Zeke smacked him upside the head before he sat on the couch. "What do you want to do tonight?"

Rex rubbed the area where he'd been hit. "Hang out at the emergency room, maybe?"

"If you need to see a doctor for that, then you really are a pussy," Zeke jabbed.

I sat on the other couch and tried to tune out their bickering.

"Maybe I'll put you in the emergency room, then," Rex threatened.

"Oh no," I said. "I think I feel a pillow fight coming on..."

They both turned to me, their eyebrows arched in annoyance.

I shrugged then turned back to the TV.

"You wanna pick up Mega Shake and play that new *Star Wars* game?" Zeke asked.

"Not a bad idea at all," Rex said. "Let me take a piss and grab my sweater." Rex walked down the hall and shut the bathroom door behind him.

Now that it was just the two of us, I felt that awkwardness again. Sometimes I swore he felt it too, but that had to be my imagination. He rested his hands on his thighs and his gaze looked into mine, the joking atmosphere evaporating like water on a hot pan. The TV wasn't on, so it was silent in the room. Even if Zeke and I were locked in a room together, we would usually be able to entertain ourselves and even have fun. But now, we didn't know how to talk to each other.

"How's Rochelle?" I thought of the first thing that came to mind, the woman in his life. They were lovey-dovey together last week, and I was surprised he wasn't with her now, or at least brought her along.

"She and I broke up, actually."

I heard what he said and knew I didn't get it wrong. It wasn't just wishful thinking and I imagined he said all of that. It really happened, and I almost couldn't believe it. "Oh. Why?" Last time I checked, they were perfectly happy.

He shrugged with a sigh. "It just didn't work out. I didn't think she was right for me." He gave me that intense gaze again, saying more with his eyes than his mouth.

"You broke up with her?"

He nodded.

"Oh...I'm so sorry."

"Thanks. But I'm okay."

I continued to stare at him because I was still in shock. How did they go from being in love to going their separate ways? "Did she do something?" Rochelle was always so thoughtful and nice. I couldn't picture her making a single wrong move.

"No." He shook his head. "I just realized we were going too fast, and I didn't see it going anywhere. I thought it was best to end it now rather than hurting her more later."

His vague response still didn't answer my question. There was something missing, but he refused to confide it to me. I left my couch and sat beside him on the other side of the room, forgetting proximity. My thigh touched his before I wrapped my arms around his neck. "I'm so sorry. I know this must be hard for you."

He paused before he moved his arms around my waist. His muscular arms dug into my sides as he gripped me tightly. He moved his face into my neck and breathed normally, his cologne flooding my nose and making me think of pine needles. "Thanks."

The hug felt amazing, like I was right at home. I could stay there forever and bask in his natural warmth. I wanted to run my hands down his back and feel the rippling muscle underneath his shirt. I wanted to get completely naked and snuggle under the sheets in my bed. I wanted to wrap my legs around his hips and feel his strength push me down into the mattress.

All that wishful thinking made me feel guilty. He just broke up with Rochelle, and all I could think about was getting him in my bed so I could make my dreams come true. I forced my hands to unclasp from around his neck so I could pull away.

While I wanted him for selfish reasons, I was more committed to being a good friend. So I said something I didn't really want to say. "Are you sure this is the right thing to do?" When I looked into his eyes, I saw his blue irises glued to my face. His hands were still around my waist and his fingers slowly loosened. "Rochelle was amazing, Zeke. She's definitely the best girl you've brought home. We all love her. Maybe you should take some time to think about it."

His voice barely came out audible. "No. I don't need to think about it."

Why did I feel like he was implying more than what he was really saying?

"I made the right decision. I have no doubts." He pulled his hands away so we weren't touching at all anymore. "I admit I'm in pain, and I'll need some time to get over our relationship. Rochelle really is a great person. But I know where I belong—and it's not with her."

He seemed certain in his decision so I didn't doubt him anymore. "I'm here if you need anything. Even if it's just someone to talk to."

His eyes narrowed with fondness. "I know."

It finally felt the way it used to, when we were friends who would do anything for each other. The conversation flowed naturally, and I felt like I was spending time with my best friend. "When Ryker and I broke up, I didn't really talk to anyone about it. I just tried not to think about him. And one day, I finally stopped thinking about him."

He nodded. "I'll try that. But I don't think Rochelle and I had the intense relationship the two of you had."

"I guess..."

He noticed my hesitation. "Do you still think about him?"

"No." The answer flew from my mouth like a bullet. Ever since I had these feelings for Zeke, I hadn't thought about anyone else. I hadn't even checked out another guy. When I saw Ryker a few weeks ago, all I felt was pity for him. I didn't want him to hold me or kiss me. My thighs didn't press together in longing. He was just a man I used to love. "I saw him the other day, and I didn't feel anything. It's strange."

"When did you see him?"

I made up a quick lie. "After work. We left the building at the same time." It was partially true. "We talked for a little bit, and he seemed really upset about his father. He said a few things about him, but then he didn't say anything else. But I could tell by his silence he was really struggling. I'd never seen him down like that. He's usually making jokes and sexual innuendos around the clock. I felt bad for him...wanted to make him feel better. But that was it. Nothing more."

Zeke stared at me intently as he listened to every word I said, hanging on to every sentence.

"It's hard to believe I was ever in love with him. It's hard to believe I'm over him. It's just...strange."

"I understand what you mean."

"While things ended so badly, I don't regret what we had. And I still remember our relationship with fondness despite the way he broke my heart. I'm just grateful I'm not bitter about it, that I can look at him and see a good person."

"Because that's who you are, Rae. You always see the good in people."

My lips automatically smiled at the compliment. "Thanks…"

"That's what I love about you."

The word he used made me shiver from my head to my toes. I understood the context of the word, but I couldn't help wishing it was used in a different way. It was painfully obvious that I was head over heels for Zeke, not just crushing on him. I wasn't sure how it got this bad. Slowly, it got worse and worse until I realized how deep I was. "And I love everything about you."

***

"He broke up with Rochelle?" Jessie nearly knocked over her glass on the table when she threw her arms into the air. "Are you serious?"

"He's single?" Kayden's hair was done in beautiful curls and she wore a dress that was almost too short. She flaunted everything she had, and every guy in the bar was staring at her. In comparison, Jessie and I looked like trolls.

"As in, totally available?" Jessie pressed. "As in, sleeping alone tonight?"

"Yeah." I felt the joy in my heart that Rochelle was gone, but then the guilt came flooding back even more intensely. "He said he realized she wasn't the right person for him. He didn't give me more information than that, unfortunately."

"That's so sudden," Kayden said. "Maybe she did something but he's covering for her. Like cheated on him or something."

"No," Jessie said. "Zeke would tell us that."

"I doubt it," Kayden argued. "He knows we would jump her."

"I can't picture Rochelle doing that," I said. "She loved him. I know she did." After I said that, I felt bad for her. She was probably home alone and crying her eyes out, just the way I used to when Ryker dumped me.

"True," Jessie admitted. "I really think she did."

"You're right," Kayden said in agreement.

"So…" Jessie smiled in that mischievous way, like she had a plan up her sleeve. "Are you gonna make a move?"

I was horrified at the thought. "Absolutely not."

"What?" Jessie said in shock. "After all those dreams and pretending to go to New York, you aren't going to ask him out? You're joking, right?"

I leaned toward her and deepened my tone. "He *just* broke up with Rochelle."

She leaned forward and made the same voice, mocking me. "*So?*"

"He's been single for, like, two days," I argued. "That's such a dick move."

"How so?" Jessie crossed her arms over her chest, pushing her cleavage line together. "If you asked him out when he was seeing Rochelle, then that would be bitchy. He's fair game if you ask me."

"Totally fair game," Kayden said. "I'd make a move right now."

"Even though he broke up with her, I doubt he's over her," I argued. "I need to give him some space before I go for it. Besides, this is Zeke we're talking about here. We're best friends. If I just asked him out, he would probably be freaked out."

"Doubtful," Jessie said. "Guys love to be hit on. Trust me."

"I'm not doing it." When Ryker dumped me, I was in no shape to start dating again, let alone dating someone I knew really well.

"Zeke is hot," Jessie reminded me. "Like Greek god hot. Someone will snatch him up if you wait too long."

"That's the chance I'm going to have to take." Just seeing him with Rochelle made me jealous. If he started seeing other girls again, I'd be heartbroken. I just wanted the chance to tell him how I felt. If he could see something happening between us, then great. But if he were looking for something else, I'd nurse my broken heart in solitude and get over him. "I'm going to give him a month. I'll see how he's doing after that. And if he looks better, I'll go for it."

"A month?" Jessie asked incredulously. "Thirty days? I've gotten over breakups quicker than that."

Kayden shrugged then sipped her drink.

"He was with Rochelle for over six months." They even said the L word to each other. This relationship was different than all the others. "Besides, I don't want to be a rebound and have a friends-with-benefits relationship. I'd get creamed just like I did with Ryker."

"Creamed is definitely the right word," Jessie said with a chuckle.

I cringed. "That has to be the dirtiest joke I've ever heard you say. Dirtier than any joke I've heard, actually."

"It fit the bill," she said with a shrug.

"So, thirty days from now…" Kayden sipped her drink. "When those thirty days are up, we're gonna be on your ass."

"Yeah, I know." I might need a little push anyway.

Kayden spotted a guy on the other side of the room. He was making eyes at her, so she was doing the same thing back. "If you'll excuse me, I'm gonna get creamed myself."

"Damn," Jessie said. "That was way dirtier than the way I said it."

"Didn't you just have a guy stay over last night?" Kayden mentioned it in passing when we were waiting for Jessie.

"Yeah." Kayden got out of the booth and placed one hand on her hip. "So?"

"It's just..." I didn't want to straight up call her a slut but...she'd kinda been acting like one.

Jessie said it in a nicer way. "It just seems like you're dating a lot more guys than you usually do...a lot more."

"I'm single," she argued. "I can do what I want."

"Yeah, but don't you think you're getting carried away?" I didn't want to hurt her feelings, but it seemed like she was throwing herself at every guy who came in her direction. Like she was in a contest neither of us knew about.

"I'm perfectly fine, thank you very much." She grabbed her clutch before she stormed off. "See you guys later. I'm gonna get some." Then she walked off, rocking her heels like sandals as she approached the next guy on her list.

Jessie watched her for a moment before she turned to me. "I'm a little worried..."

"Me too."

"What do you think has gotten into her?"

I shrugged. "I know as much as you do."

Ray of Love

Chapter Thirteen

Rae

I didn't see Zeke for a week.

Now that he was single, I was terrified he would bring some other woman around, and I would miss my chance—for the second time. Since he was unencumbered, my sex dreams turned insanely erotic. We were doing it all over the place—my bed, the shower, even the hallway outside my apartment.

He was making me come so often I didn't need a man—or a vibrator.

But now I didn't feel guilty for having my fantasies. He wasn't committed to Rochelle anymore, so technically, I wasn't doing anything wrong. In the middle of the day, when Rex wasn't home from work, I whipped out my vibrator and pictured the way Zeke looked shirtless on the basketball court.

That sight would hold me over for weeks.

Instead of feeling dirty for my actions, I felt more attached to him. It seemed like I was already in a strange and twisted relationship with him even though he wasn't aware of it. I knew I sounded like a crazy nutcase, but when it came to Zeke, I was okay with being a little crazy.

On Friday after work, he texted me. *Want to play some ball?*

I nearly fell off my bed when I saw that message. Instead of playing it cool, I immediately texted him back. *Sure. When?*

Twenty minutes.

I'll meet you there.

K.

My heart accelerated with a spike of adrenaline. The nerves burned in my gut, and the anxiety reminded me how I felt anytime I went on a first date. It wasn't a date at all, just two friends playing basketball.

But to me, it was so much more.

I hoped he'd take off his shirt.

The weather was nice—clear and sunny.

My odds were good.

***

I took Safari with me because I knew he was eager to get outside. My apartment wasn't the best place for him. One day, I would get a house, and he would run around the backyard, pooping on the grass and claiming it as his own.

When I reached the court, Zeke was already there practicing his shots.

And he was shirtless.

This day just got so damn good.

He made the shot then grabbed the ball before it rolled away. He flashed me his perfect smile, nothing but straight teeth in a ridiculously handsome face, and then tucked the ball into his side. "Hey. It's my favorite person in the world."

"I'm your favorite person?" Now I couldn't stop myself from smiling.

"I was talking about Safari." When he chuckled, even that sounded sexy. "But you come in a close second." He winked.

And that wink made me melt.

Seriously, how did I not notice him before?

He was sexy. Like, obviously sexy. He was sweet and charming. He was smart and compassionate. And his body...wow. Everything about him was just perfect. Why did I date all those losers when I could have just dated Zeke instead?

Biggest mistake.

I recovered from the warmth that flooded my cheeks. "At least I made the list."

"You're always on the list, Rae." He kneeled and gave Safari a good rub-down, scratching him behind the ears then running his hands down his back. "How's my man?"

Safari panted with sleepy eyes, enjoying the massage he was getting.

"He needed some fresh air. Thought he could ref the game."

"That's not fair," Zeke said. "He'll be totally biased."

"Against you?"

"Actually, against you." Zeke rose to his full height, his body glistening with sweat from the mini workout he just completed on the court. That smile was back, the corner of his lips rising in a mischievous way.

"You're cocky today." Without thinking, I dug my hands into his side and tickled him.

He laughed from deep in his throat and stepped back, protecting his physique from my prying fingers. "I'm always cocky."

My fingers could barely tickle him because I felt like I was touching steel. "We'll see just how cocky you are after I kick your ass."

"I distinctly remember you getting your ass handed to you a few weeks ago."

"Well, that was because—" I shut my mouth before I said something stupid. "I was a little sick."

"Whatever you say..."

We started the game and both put in our best effort. Zeke was fast, having the momentum from his speed and size, and when he zoomed past me, there wasn't much I could do to stop him. He scored on me then handed the ball over. "Not a good start."

"Shut up and let's play."

He grinned. "You've never liked losing."

I dribbled the ball past him and sprinted to the opposite hoop. Zeke was on me instantly, his perfect body covering all my open shots. He threw his arms in the air before I could throw the ball. His chest was like the wall to a building—there was no way through.

But I didn't really want to get around it. I wanted to go through it, feel my nails drag down his chest and his stomach. I wanted to touch those ripped arms as they pumped with blood. I didn't even want to play basketball. I wanted to push him to his back and ride him right then and there.

His body distracted me, and before I knew it, he stole the ball from me. "No!"

Zeke sprinted to the opposite side and made the shot. "Looks like you just got scored on—again."

I wish that were also true outside the game. "You got lucky."

"Being a better ballplayer isn't luck. It's fact."

I narrowed my eyes at him. "Hand me the ball, and we'll see who the better player is."

***

Zeke beat me—fair and square.

But in my defense, it was hard to concentrate when he was shirtless and sexy. No wonder why all the players in the NBA wore shirts. It would be too damn distracting for everyone involved.

Like the gentleman he was, Zeke didn't gloat. "You wanna get some food at Mega Shake?"

"I could use a greasy burger and even greasier fries…"

He grabbed his shirt from the ground and started to pull it on.

"No!"

He stopped just before he pulled it over his head. He gave me a blank stare, unsure what my outburst meant.

Shit, I said that out loud? "Thought there was a spider…"

He pulled it on the rest of the way, hiding his perfect chest and ripped stomach.

I sighed like I'd never be happy again.

Zeke whistled. "Come on, boy. Let's get some food."

Safari immediately jumped up and came to his side.

Together, we walked a few blocks before we entered the restaurant. Safari sat outside with his leash tied to a pole. He was in a shady spot near the door, and customers patted him on the head as they came and went.

We washed our hands, ordered, and then took a seat with our trays of food.

I reminded myself he couldn't eat shirtless inside the restaurant, so that ending was unlikely. But if he were spending the night in my room, he would've been shirtless all the time... That was a nice thought.

"What are you smiling about?"

"Huh?" I flinched at his observation, not even knowing I was smiling.

He finished chewing his bite of food before he repeated the question. "You were grinning out of nowhere. Just curious as to why."

"Oh...I remembered a joke I heard at work today."

"I didn't know Jenny was the joke-making type."

"She has her moments..." I looked down at my food and threw a few fries into my mouth.

Zeke fell into silence as he ate, taking big bites and devouring his food like most men I knew. Somehow, he made the action sexy. He opened his wide jaw and chewed quickly, his eyes on his meal. When he got a little sauce in the corner, he wiped it away with his thumb before he sucked it off.

God, I couldn't last thirty days.

I wanted to ask him out right then and there.

And if he said no, I'd probably still ask him if he wanted to hook up. After months with my dreams and my vibrator, I needed the real thing. "How's work?" I blurted it out just so we had something boring and unsexual to talk about.

"It was good. I have a patient diagnosed with skin cancer. But we were able to remove the affected tissue, and he's doing well. I think we stopped it before it spread."

"That's good to hear." I loved hearing how involved Zeke was with his work. He really cared about his patients and doing the right thing for them. His paycheck seemed to be the last thing on his mind. He was booked months in advance because everyone knew he was the best dermatologist in the state. He wasn't just knowledgeable, but he had the kind of compassion you didn't see too often.

Why the hell didn't I notice him before?

I could have asked him out when he had feelings for me.

We'd be fucking right now.

But I went out with Ryker instead…the guy who broke my heart.

Zeke would never do that to me.

The sadness hit me hard, and I was so depressed I thought I would never be happy again.

Zeke picked up on my mood, having a sixth sense. "Everything alright?"

"Yeah, of course. I just feel bad for your patient. Must have been scary."

"Yeah, it can be traumatic. But at least he'll be alright. How's work for you?"

"It's pretty good. About the same."

He dunked his fries into his ketchup before he shoved them into his mouth. "So…have you been seeing anyone?"

"Of course not." The words flew out of my mouth like word vomit. I regretted it the moment it happened and wished I could take it back. But now it was out there…in the air. "I just… No. I haven't been seeing anyone." There was only one guy I wanted in my bed. He just became available a week ago, but I had to keep my hands to myself. "You?"

Please say no.

Please say no.

Please say no.

"No," he answered. "I've been spending a lot of time at the house, mainly playing video games."

Oh, thank god. If he hooked up with a former lover for a rebound, I'd be sick to my stomach. "What game?"

"That race car game Rex and I play."

"Cool."

He paused before he spoke. "Rochelle came over to pick up her things yesterday..."

I immediately felt guilty for lusting after him when she was going through such a hard time. She just lost the greatest guy in the world. No one could swallow that well. "How is she?"

"The same. She asked if we could give the relationship another try."

My heart stopped beating. "Oh..." Did he say yes?

"I said no. And that made her cry all over again." He sighed before he kept eating. "I feel so fucking terrible for hurting her. She doesn't deserve it. I wish...I wish I could make her forget me."

"No...she would never want to do that." Despite what Ryker did to me, I didn't regret what we had. I really loved him, and even when he walked away from me, I still felt that way. It was a shame it didn't lead to forever, but even a few months with him was better than no time at all. "She may feel terrible now, but it will pass. One day, she'll remember you with joy. She just needs time to get there."

"Is that how you think of Ryker?"

I nodded. "Yeah. Seeing him in agony over his father's passing breaks my heart. And I know I feel that way because I loved him. Once you love someone once, you kinda always feel differently toward them than you do everyone else. I'll always care about him and want the best for him. I don't think about the way he hurt me anymore. I just...see him for who he is."

"I understand what you mean."

"She'll get through it, Zeke. Don't feel too bad."

"I guess..." He took another bite of his burger.

"Unless you do want to be with her..."

"I don't." He said it before he even finished chewing. Once he swallowed, he continued on. "The past week and a half has only convinced me I made the right decision." He held my gaze for a long moment before he finally blinked and looked away. "I just wish she hadn't taken it so hard. I'll always care about her and want the best for her too. But I can't be with her anymore."

He never told me the reason why he broke up with her. I just hoped he gave her a good enough explanation. "Did you just wake up one morning and think of her differently?"

"I guess." He didn't elaborate.

"Maybe that's why she's taking it so hard...because it's not a concrete reason."

"Maybe," he said. "But I made it clear my heart isn't in it anymore. I think I got her hopes up when I told her she was my longest and most serious relationship. I shouldn't have moved so fast... I should have slowed down."

"You did what felt right at the time. Shouldn't regret that."

"I suppose." He finished his food then wiped his fingers with a napkin.

"Rochelle will find someone else. She's a great woman."

"I know she will," he said with a sigh. "I just hope it happens sooner rather than later."

I ate the last of my fries and fought the urge to make up an excuse to go to his place. With the trees surrounding the house and his dark furniture and art lights on the walls, it was a romantic place. Maybe he could see me as something other than a friend again. I wasn't sure how to make that happen. I wasn't even sure what attracted him to me in the first place. "Do you have any plans for the rest of the day?"

"Just playing a video game when I get home."

"Well, the Mariners game is on. You wanna watch that?" I didn't want to invite him to my apartment because my piece of shit brother didn't understand the meaning of get out.

"Sounds like an excellent idea. Want to come to my place?"

Like we had the same mind, he did exactly what I wanted. "Sure. I'll swing by my place and change."

"Okay. But then Rex is going to want to join us."

Did he want to be alone with me? "And what's the problem with that?"

"Nothing. I just figured you'd want some space from him."

"I do," I blurted. "I really want some space from him."

"Then you can shower at my place and wear some of my stuff."

A fantasy come true—wearing his t-shirt around his house. "Okay..." I couldn't keep the excitement from escaping my voice. Maybe I could even get a peek of him in the shower if I were sneaky enough.

"Besides, Safari loves my backyard." He glanced at him through the window.

"He does."

He piled our trash together. "Ready to go?"

"Absolutely."

***

Zeke got into the shower first while I sat on the couch and watched the game.

I texted Jessie. *Zeke and I played basketball today, and now I'm at his place...just the two of us.*

The three dots popped up immediately. *Jump. His. Bones.*

I can't. That's why I'm texting you. My hormones are all over the place right now. I need you to talk some sense into me.

Then you texted the wrong person, amiga.

Jessie!

Get that D, girl.

You're so not helping right now.

I'm helping you get laid.

I locked my screen so I couldn't see her messages anymore. That pep talk was completely counterproductive. Now I wanted to retire my vibrator and use Zeke full time. I looked out the window and saw Safari sitting in the grass, loving the outdoors. I knew we would both like to live there if we had the opportunity.

Now I was getting ahead of myself.

Zeke came out in his running shorts and a t-shirt. His hair was still damp from the shower, and he was clean and masculine. He set a towel and a stack of clothes on the couch. "Here you go. Need anything else?"

I was hoping he'd come down the hall with a towel around his waist. That's how it happened in books, so why didn't that happen to me right now? Not fair at all. "No, I'm good. Thank you."

"Alright. I'll be waiting." He sat on the couch and picked up his beer.

I went into the bathroom and shut the door behind me. I'd never showered in his house before. In fact, I'd never been there overnight. Even though my apartment was small and cramped, everyone came to hang out there.

I turned on the water and got underneath the faucet. The warm water blanketed me like a cocoon. I spotted his body wash on the rack, along with his shampoo. The place was touched by his presence, and I pictured him in the shower, the water falling against his hard chest.

I'd been hard up all day and nothing was chasing away my desperation. Maybe I could think clearly if I released the tension between my legs. Feeling dirty but also excited, I touched myself in his shower and pictured him in there with me.

After a few minutes, I released, thinking about him the entire time. I managed to stay quiet, and the water muffled the sounds I made. I'd never masturbated in someone else's house, but the urge overtook me and I couldn't fight it.

And I felt a lot better once I was finished.

After I dried off, I went back into the living room.

"Feel better?"

"What?" Fuck, did he know?

"You know, now that you're clean. What did you think I meant?"

"I just..." My cheeks had turned beet red, and they were slowly fading back to their original color. "I really like your shampoo."

"Head & Shoulders?"

"Yeah...I guess I have dandruff." I sat on the opposite side of the couch and pulled my knees to my chest. "So, the Mariners are winning, huh?" I had to change the subject of that conversation—pronto.

"Yeah. Just scored another run." He turned back to the TV and drank his beer.

Now that his attention was off me, I could finally breathe again.

Ray of Love

Chapter Fourteen

Rex

I thought I would get better as time went by, but I seemed to be getting worse.

All I could think about was Kayden and who she was spending the night with. I ended our arrangement because Zeke told me I should so she wouldn't get attached. But now I was wondering if I was the one who got attached.

Did I?

I hadn't been with anyone else since Kayden, and a month had come and gone without any action. It was the longest dry spell I'd ever experienced, and the fact that it was voluntary made it more unusual.

So I decided to hit the bar scene and scoop up a date. Maybe I just needed to get back in the game, and I would stop thinking about Kayden. She clearly had already moved on, and I needed to do the same.

I sat at the bar and looked around, but I didn't see anyone worth my interest. There was just a sea of legs and big hair. I stared down into my beer most of the time. After nearly half an hour of nothing, I paid my tab and prepared to leave.

And that's when I saw her.

Kayden walked inside wearing a tight black dress. Her blonde hair was straight, and black diamond earrings were in her lobes. Like a vision, she made everything in the background look like an indistinct blur.

I couldn't stop looking at her.

She scanned the bar like she was looking for someone. Then her eyes settled on me, full of surprise.

I stared back and didn't know what else to do. I suddenly felt nervous and uneasy. We hadn't had a real conversation since we broke up a month ago. My attempt to bring her soup backfired. I ended up talking to her through a tiny crack in the doorway before she dismissed me.

She regained her confidence and closed the gap between us. "Hi."

"Hi." She looked so pretty that I wanted to grip her by the shoulders and kiss her. But I chickened out and chose to stare at her instead. "You look beautiful tonight."

Her cheeks immediately tinted. "Thank you..."

Could I ask her to fool around again? Or had I said goodbye to that possibility the second I ended things with her? "It's nice to see you. I feel like we never talk anymore."

"I know what you mean. I've just been busy."

Dating every guy in the world. "Yeah..."

"What have you been up to?"

"You know, just work and stuff." And playing a lot of video games and hanging out with Zeke.

"Cool."

"How's the library?"

"Good."

Awkward silence fell.

I came out tonight to pick up someone and bring them back to my place. But now that I was looking at her, I realized I didn't want to find anyone else. I wanted her on my bed with her legs wrapped around my waist. I wanted her to be the one to say my name when I made her come. "I know this is crazy but—"

"Hey, babe." A good-looking guy in a collared shirt appeared out of nowhere and wrapped his arm around her waist. "You look fantastic tonight."

"Oh, thanks." She tucked her hair behind her ear. "You look nice too."

Vomit formed in my stomach.

"Can I get you a drink?" Judging the way he pretended I didn't exist, he considered me to be a threat. He probably saw me checking her out before he was able to claim her as his.

"Yeah, sure," she said. "By the way, this is my friend Rex."

Her friend Rex.

Just her friend.

Some guy who she didn't think about anymore.

I forced myself to be polite. "Nice to meet you…"

He glared at me like I was scum. "Yeah, you too."

"See you later, Rex." Kayden drifted away with her date, hitting the bar for some booze and fun.

I stood there and watched them disappear, feeling out of place in the world. The last thing I should feel was jealousy or regret. I was the one who called it off before things could get serious. Kayden had every right to do what she was doing—living her life.

But I felt like shit anyway.

***

When I walked through the door, I tossed my keys on the counter. But I was so disturbed by the sight of Kayden with that guy that I missed the surface and tossed them on the floor. They fell with a distinct clank when they hit the tile.

Rae was sitting at the kitchen table on her computer, probably doing some work after hours.

Once in a while, she brought her work home with her when she didn't finish in the lab. It was usually calculations. "What's up with you?"

I snatched the keys from the ground and tossed them on the counter. This time, I didn't miss. "Nothing."

"You're home by nine." She gave me that annoying know-it-all sister look. "Something must be up."

"Nothing good out tonight."

"Yeah, okay," she said with a chuckle. "When I was out with Jessie the other night, I saw this woman who was so beautiful she made Jessie look like a troll. There's a lot of talent out on the town. Did someone shoot you down?"

Pretty much. "Not really. I sat at the bar by myself for a few hours then came home."

"Wow...that's depressing."

She didn't know the half of it. "I saw Kayden...with some guy." It hurt to say the words out loud. I could have been spending the night with her. But instead, I was going to bed alone and suffering through my nightmares.

Rae sighed like a speech was approaching. "I'm worried about her. Out with a different guy every night...it's just not like her."

A different guy every night? Now I really felt sick.

"I've never seen her date more than two guys a year. And now she's probably seen twenty in the last month. She says everything is fine but it's hard to believe. Right after she was done being sick, she went on this sexy rampage—"

"I'm going to bed." I couldn't hear any more of that. My heart was ripping in two, and I wanted to jump off a cliff. Just seeing her with some other guy was disgusting, but knowing there had been dozens after me was just cruel. "Good night."

Ray of Love

Chapter Fifteen

Rae

My phone lit up with a text message when I was at work. I was sitting at the desk against the wall, jotting down notes so I wouldn't forget this information later. Zeke's name popped up on the screen, and I almost jumped on the table and started dancing. *Hungry?*

He was asking me to lunch! *Really? Do you even need to ask?*

Forgot I was talking to a bottomless pit.

I sent an emoji of me giving him the bird.

He sent an emoji of a grinning face. *Pizza?*

I'm always down for pizza.

I finished up my project in the lab before I walked a few blocks over and met him at the pizza parlor we always went to. He was already sitting in the booth with the pizza in front of him—knowing what I would want without even asking.

"This looks bomb." I sat across from him and immediately pulled a slice onto my plate.

"I almost got started without you but I'm too much of a gentleman."

"You know I wouldn't care. I wouldn't wait for you."

He chuckled, looking undeniably handsome with that smile. "You're right."

"So, how's work?" I ate and looked at him across the table, feeling my thighs press together because he looked so sexy when he wore dark blue. He looked sexy in every color, but his scrubs had a sharp V-neck in the front, and I could see the line that separated the two pec muscles.

"Good. I'm considering hiring another dermatologist and expanding the business a little."

"Oh, that's cool. Maybe open another office too?"

"No, I'm not that ambitious. I actually wanted to split the load with someone so I could have more time off. Right now, I'm so swamped that I can't take a vacation. I can't even remember the last time I took a day off besides the weekends."

"True. Don't overwork yourself."

"Yeah, that's why I think I'm going to hire someone. We'll have to take on more clients, but that shouldn't be a problem. We have people booked nine months out right now."

"That's crazy."

"I know. People shouldn't wait that long to be seen."

"Why don't they just go somewhere else?"

He shrugged. "I don't know. It might be an insurance issue."

I'd never understood insurance and I never would.

"I take all kinds of insurance, even the ones that don't pay much. That probably has something to do with it."

I think I just fell a little harder for him. "That's sweet of you…"

"The way I see it is, I grew up with food, shelter, and health insurance. And now I have a great job that provides all the things I need. Some people don't have that kind of luxury. It's not their fault. Sometimes, they just got dealt a bad hand. So the least I can do is help people who can't help themselves. I mean, I'm a doctor. That's the definition of my occupation."

I wanted to jump his bones right then and there. He was so humble and so compassionate. I never met a man who cared so much for people less fortunate. He was so swoon-worthy, and I was definitely being swooned. "We're lucky to have you, Dr. Collins."

He smiled before he took a bite of his pizza. "Well, thanks."

I wanted to reach across the table and hug him, but I knew nothing good would come of that. He would feel the hardness of my tits. And when I straddled his hips, that would be a dead giveaway of what I really wanted.

"Anything new at the lab?" His question cooled the heat between my legs.

"I'm working on a few things. Biodegradable products for consumers. Finding the right expiration time is the most difficult part. Can't seem to get that right."

"I can't even imagine how complicated that is."

"And I can't imagine how complicated medical school is."

"It's not that bad, actually. You could do it. A monkey could do it."

"Okay, I could probably do it," I said. "But a monkey?"

"Yeah." He said it with a straight face. "It's like playing detective. Someone has a problem and you solve it. There are different tools you use to figure it out. Once you have that data, you make a decision on how to fix the problem. It's straightforward."

In my eyes, he was definitely downplaying it. But for someone so intelligent, it wasn't surprising that he considered the challenge easy. "Do you have plans tonight?"

"No. Just playing video games."

"You must have beaten that racing one by now."

He shrugged. "You can't really beat it. That's just for fun. But I did finish the first shooter game. Pretty cool. Do you have plans tonight?"

"Sorta." I'd been concerned about Kayden for a while, and it was time for me to seriously confront her. "I'm worried about Kayden."

"Because?"

"She's been sleeping around a lot, and I'm just concerned."

Zeke's expression didn't change. "I don't see what the problem is. She's single and can do whatever she wants."

"But it's just not like her to do that sort of thing."

He shrugged. "I feel like if she were a man, no one would raise an eyebrow. But since she's a woman, there must be something wrong."

I loved Zeke for being a feminist. He was always a gentleman and treated women right, but he also saw them as equals. That might be the sexiest thing of all about him. "That's not what I'm implying at all."

"Then is there something you aren't telling me?"

"No...but her sudden change in behavior started after she was done being sick. It was just night and day, such a sudden shift that Jessie and I could hardly believe it. I wonder if there's something she's not telling me."

"I guess it doesn't hurt to ask."

"I mean, if she's really fine and is just changing her lifestyle, good for her. But I've known her my whole life, and I just feel like something is wrong."

Zeke nodded. "You know her better than anyone, so your hunch is probably right."

"After work, I'm going to confront her. I just hope she takes it well. Last time I said something, she got a little defensive."

"That's a natural reaction," he said. "You know, when someone questions your behavior."

"Yeah..." I moved on to my third slice until I was stuffed. I couldn't eat another bite if someone paid me.

Zeke watched me from across the table, his beautiful blue eyes brilliant and seductive. I loved it when he stared at me because I got to stare back. I saw the wisdom and the sexiness in his expression. With his hard jaw and soft lips, he looked like a fantasy. He was single and totally available, but I couldn't do a damn thing to make him mine. I had to wait a little longer out of respect for our friendship.

But who knew being a good friend could be so damn hard.

***

Kayden opened the door, her hair and makeup done like she was about to go out.

Even though it was Monday.

Who went out on a Monday night? I was usually parked in front of my TV with sweats and a beanie, hating the fact I had to get through the rest of the week before the weekend arrived again.

"Oh, hey. What's up?" She invited me inside, her feet bare because her heels were the only thing missing from her outfit. "What's up? Anything happen with Zeke yet?"

"No. But my thirty days aren't up yet."

"Whatever." She rolled her eyes. "The thirty-day rule is stupid and you know it."

I sat on the couch. "Going out?"

"Yeah, you wanna come?" A glass of wine was sitting on the table, next to a full bottle.

"No. Actually, I was hoping we could talk."

Kayden detected my tone immediately. She looked at me with suspicion, knowing something bad was coming. "Talk about what?"

She was going to hate me for saying this—I knew it. "With all the guys you've been seeing and how much you go out...I'm still a little worried. I feel like there's something else going on but you aren't telling me what it is."

She laughed it off. "You're reading way too much into it, Rae. I'm not a science experiment to analyze."

"I'm not analyzing you. But I've known you since we were five. You've been exactly the same person since that time. And all of a sudden...you just changed. I'm just concerned something more serious is going on."

"I haven't changed," she argued. "I just got some confidence, and I like to go out. That's all."

Since she was defensive, I knew she was hiding something. But it was a mystery why she kept it a secret. "I don't care about you going out and having a good time. I'm more concerned about all the men you've been sleeping with."

"You're one to talk," she scoffed. "You've picked up tons of guys from bars."

"I know I have." I wasn't ashamed of it. "But it wasn't a different guy every night. Before Ryker came into the picture, I slept with five guys in one year. That's reasonable. But what you're doing...is concerning."

"You're calling me a slut?" she hissed.

"No. I never said that word."

"It's pretty clear you're implying it."

I lowered my tone so she would remain calm. "Listen to me. If you're doing this because you want to do it, that's fine. I won't say another word about it. But if you're doing this because something happened to you, something bad, then I think we should talk about it. That's all. So, Kayden, has anything happened in the past month?"

She stared me down, and slowly, her anger started to fade away. Her eyebrows began to soften and the look in her eyes was no longer fierce. She morphed back into the woman I knew, my friend.

I hit a nerve.

Kayden remained quiet. Her eyes drifted down to her untouched wine glass.

"Kayden, you know you can tell me anything. You've always been there for me. Let me be there for you."

She interlocked her fingers and sighed. "You're going to be mad…"

"Why would I be mad?"

"Because I did something that kind of breaks the girl code."

I didn't have a clue what she was talking about. "I promise I won't be mad."

"You can't make a promise like that."

"Honestly, I couldn't care less about what you did. Right now, all I care about is you. There's nothing you could say to make me turn on you. Even if you slept with Ryker, while it would hurt, I wouldn't be mad because that doesn't matter right now. Only you matter."

Her eyes softened with sadness. "Rae, I would never do that."

My heart relaxed in relief. I was over Ryker, but if one of my friends slept with him, I would be devastated. "I know. But anything you actually did do would pale in comparison to that. So just tell me."

"Alright..."

I stared her down as I anxiously waited.

"This is hard to talk about...so I'm just going to come out and say it."

"Okay."

"I've been in love with Rex for years now."

I heard what she said, but I couldn't process it. Her confession was huge—enormous. I didn't even suspect she had a thing for my brother. Not once had it crossed my mind. Since she was staring at me, I knew I needed to say something. "Oh…"

"I kept hoping he would notice me the way I noticed him. But of course, he only saw me as a friend. So I did something really stupid and…I asked him to teach me some moves in the bedroom. I thought if we fooled around long enough, he would want to be with me." She lowered her gaze and stared at her hands, not wanting to look me in the eye. "But then he broke up with me a month ago. Didn't say why. He just said our arrangement was over. And…it hurt so much." She closed her eyes, and tears immediately began to leak out.

The shock of what happened between her and Rex passed in light of her pain. I went to her side on the couch and wrapped my arms around her, pulling her into me so I could comfort my best friend in the world. "Kayden…"

She rested her head on my shoulder. "I know I shouldn't be crying. I know I should have seen what was coming. But...I really love him, Rae."

I rubbed her back, feeling heartbroken for her. "I know you do, Kay." I didn't need to question her feelings to know it was true. Seeing her break down in front of me like this, hitting rock bottom, was proof enough. I didn't have time to feel the confusion of everything she just said. A part of me was surprised I hadn't figured it out on my own since she'd felt this way for so long. Jessie didn't have a clue either.

"I'm sorry I slept with Rex. I know he's your brother and everything..."

"Don't worry about it." I continued to rub her back, not feeling any resentment toward her whatsoever. She didn't just mess with my brother's feelings. She was the one who loved him, and he didn't feel the same way. "Did he know you felt this way?"

"I don't think so," she whispered. "I guess I did a good job of hiding it."

"So, when you were sick...?"

"I was just depressed."

"Oh, sweetie..." I rubbed her shoulder.

"I've been going out a lot lately to make myself feel better...to forget about him. I don't want him to know how much he hurt me because he wouldn't care anyway. And I was hoping I could get over him if I met enough guys. But nothing seems to work..."

"I know how hard it is. Believe me, Kay. I do." Getting over Ryker was the hardest thing I'd ever had to do. He was the love of my life, the man I pictured myself spending the rest of my life with. When I pictured my husband's face, it was Ryker. But when I told him I loved him, he broke my heart. He threw me aside like trash and moved on with his life, leaving me in the dust. Those three months were unbearable.

"I know you do, Rae. I'm just sorry that you do understand."

I lowered my hand from her back. "I know you're in pain, but I don't think sleeping around is going to make you feel better, Kayden. I think you need to confront these feelings head on, as painful as it is, and slowly move on."

She sniffed then wiped her eyes. "I know..."

"And when you feel better, you'll find someone really special and fall in love. Rex will miss the greatest thing that ever happened to him, and you'll be happy with someone who actually deserves you."

She nodded. "I hope you're psychic, Rae."

"I don't need to be psychic to know that's going to happen. You deserve the best. And one day, you'll get it."

She finally stopped crying, her eyes becoming dry. She sat up and looked at me, the plea in her gaze. "Don't say anything to Rex, okay?"

I didn't say anything.

"Rae," she pressed.

"I think you should tell him how you feel. I promise, he has no clue that you feel this way."

"How do you know?"

"Believe me, I just do. Rex is dull when it comes to stuff like this. He's a smart guy, but when it comes to reading people's emotions and attitudes, he's totally blind. He believed whatever you told him, and as far as he's concerned, you couldn't care less about him."

"I don't know..."

"If you want a chance to be with him, I think you should tell him. You'll never know until you try."

She shook her head. "I want him to want me on his own. I want him to chase me and try to win me over. I don't want to be just some girl he fools around with. I want him to love me the way I love him. And if I have to tell him how I feel to make that happen...then it's not real."

"I understand that...but Rex doesn't know any of that."

"And I don't want to come out and say it. I know he doesn't feel the same way and things will just be awkward. At least we can be friends now. That's never been an issue, thankfully."

Seeing my friend in pain hurt my heart. I wanted to fix it, but I didn't know how.

"So let's just keep this between us, okay?"

"Alright." I agreed with her just for the sake of it. While I understood where she was coming from, I didn't think she was going about it in the right way. If Rex thought they were only fooling around, that's all he would ever feel. You needed to be direct with him if you wanted any kind of response.

"Thank you. And again, I'm sorry."

"Don't apologize, Kayden. I'm just glad you finally let me in. I want to help you get better, and now I can finally do that."

She smiled for the first time. "Thanks, Rae. You're such a good friend."

"Best friend," I corrected. "And you don't need to thank me."

Ray of Love

Chapter Sixteen

Rae

I couldn't look at Rex the same way.

I walked into the apartment after staying at Kayden's place for a few hours. Instead of going out, we watched a few movies on the couch. She put on her pajamas and returned to her normal self, a homebody who preferred the company of close friends rather than handsome strangers.

Rex was sitting on the couch watching a basketball game. A collection of beer bottles sat on the table before him. Like a slug, he sat there and hardly moved.

I couldn't believe he fooled around with my best friend for so long—and hid it so well.

And I couldn't believe he would mess with my friend like that.

I walked into the living room and crossed my arms over my chest.

Rex glanced at me. "What's your problem?" His eyes turned back to the TV, and that's when I noticed just how down he was. When he came home the other night, he was in a terrible mood. And that mood hadn't gone away since.

"I should ask you the same thing."

"Just tired. What's your excuse?"

Sick of your bullshit, that's what. "You've been weird since the other day. Something up?"

"No." He took a long drink of his beer and continued to ignore me.

There was no point in feeling him out. He wouldn't tell me a damn thing. "Good night, then."

"Where were you?"

"Kayden's." I was just about to turn away when I decided to stay put.

His movements were slight, but he changed the tension in his shoulders and shifted his weight on the couch. And the biggest clue of all, he looked at me.

"What did you guys do? Did you go out? Did she pick up another guy?"

A lot of questions from someone who wasn't supposed to care. "No. We stayed at her place and watched TV. Why?"

His mood picked up slightly. His eyes dilated like he heard something he liked. He turned back to the TV and took another drink of his beer. "Just asking to be polite."

"But you're never polite."

"Then I was just asking."

"Or are you actually curious?" I pressed.

"I don't know," he said with a shrug.

Now that I looked back on our past conversations, he did show particular interest whenever Kayden was involved. He always asked if she was coming to events, and when I mentioned she was sleeping around, he marched off to bed. Maybe there was more to this story than Kayden and I both realized.

Maybe.

***

I left the building and started the walk back to my place. I pulled out my phone and called Zeke. I wasn't just reaching out to him for an excuse to talk to him. He was one of my best friends, and I needed to tell someone about this huge piece of news.

He answered immediately. "Long time, no see."

"Are you off work?"

"Just got home and out of the shower."

Damn, I missed the show. "I need to talk to you. I have some ridiculously big news. Can I come over?" And please still be in a towel when I get there.

"Absolutely. The front door is open."

"Alright. See you soon."

"I'll order a pizza. You're probably starving." The teasing tone was in his voice.

I smiled automatically, turned on by that simple joke. The banter between us felt so much more flirtatious now that I wanted to hit his sheets. Of course, it made me blush. "Good call."

***

When I walked in, the pizza was already there. Zeke wasn't in a towel, unfortunately. He was dressed in jeans and a t-shirt, the kind with a V-neck down the front. It wasn't as prominent as the one in his scrubs, but I could still see the definition of muscle around his collarbone.

"So, what's the big news?" He grabbed a beer from the fridge, opened it for me, and left it on the table so I could grab it whenever I wanted.

I always opened my own beer, and I thought it was strange he did it for me. I sat down and pulled the beer toward me but didn't take a drink. With my news, there wouldn't be time for drinking or eating. "Rex was never seeing a woman named Bonnie."

Zeke pulled a slice onto his plate but didn't take a bite. His attention turned back to me. "What are you getting at?"

"Last night, Kayden told me she and Rex were fooling around for a while. Basically, they were fuck buddies."

Judging by the way Zeke's eyes expanded to twice their size, he had no clue. "Are you serious?"

"Dead serious."

"Are you sure?"

"Kayden wouldn't make that up."

Flustered, he ran his fingers through his hair like a sexy model who just got out of the pool. "Wow...that's insane."

"I guess it lasted a long time, a few months."

"I can't believe Rex would be so stupid as to get involved with a friend like that."

The hope died in my chest when I heard what he said. Did that mean he would never want to date me because we were good friends? That the risk to our friendship outweighed our attraction?

"I can't believe I never noticed. They seemed so normal around each other."

"I couldn't believe it either. Kayden explained that's why she's sleeping around with every guy she sees."

"Because?"

Did I need to spell it out for him? "She's in love with him. She told me she's been in love with him for years. She thought if they started a physical relationship, he would see her as more than just a friend. But he ended it one day and that was it."

"She had feelings for him all this time?"

I nodded.

"And none of us knew?"

"I guess so. She's heartbroken over the whole thing. I told her she needs to focus on getting better, not sleeping with every man in Seattle."

"All the men in Seattle will be disappointed," he said with a chuckle.

I narrowed my eyes.

"Other than me," he said quickly. "I don't see Kayden like that and never have." His voice came out defensive, even a little paranoid. "So does Rex know?"

He didn't need to ask that to get my answer. "No. He's clueless."

"I guess that doesn't surprise me."

"She asked me not to say anything, and I guess I won't...but I've noticed how down he's been lately. He's been withdrawn and sad, and sometimes I wonder if it's because of her. Maybe he's just as miserable with this breakup as she is."

"Maybe. I remember talking to him about it when I thought the woman was named Bonnie. I said he should end it before things became serious. He would just hurt her in the end. But it didn't seem like he really wanted to shake her."

"Maybe he didn't."

"But he seemed adamant about her not getting attached...which makes me think he's not serious about her."

Unfortunately. "I think I'm going to tell him anyway."

"You sure you want to do that?"

"Yeah. I want him to understand how much he hurt my friend with his stupid decision to use her. And if he does have deeper feelings for her, I want him to understand she feels the same way so he can do something about it."

Zeke was quiet, telling me he disagreed.

"She doesn't want him to know because if he does chase after her, it's only because I talked him into it. If he comes to her on his own terms, then she'll know it's real. But what she doesn't get is, Rex is totally dense about these sorts of things. He's not good at reading people and understanding emotions. You really have to spell stuff out for him. And even then, he doesn't totally get it either."

"True." Zeke grabbed his slice and took a bite. "So I have to act like I don't know anything?"

"Until I talk to him."

"Let me know when you do. Because I want to give him an earful."

I actually felt bad for my brother.

He answered my unspoken question. "I'm his best friend. He should have told me about this."

"Kayden is my best friend, but she didn't tell me either. So you're in good company."

"Anytime I'm with you, I'm in good company." He took another bite and chewed like he didn't just say something that could make me melt. He had moves without even trying. Or maybe it was just because I was so head over heels that everything he said made my heart burn with hope.

***

"I need to talk to you." I grabbed the remote and turned off the TV.

"You know what?" Rex sat up and glared at me. "I'm really tired of the way you barge in all the time."

"Into my own living room?"

"Well, you don't need to turn off the TV," he said defensively. "I'm watching the game."

"There's always a game on, Rex. You can't watch them all." I sat on the other couch and tossed my purse aside.

"Then hurry up and spit it out so I can get back to it."

"I know about you and Kayden." I just came out and said it, being blunt about it. There was no good way to start this conversation, and there also wasn't a bad way to start it either. No matter what, it would be awkward.

Rex kept his expression exactly the same, giving nothing away. "That we're friends and nothing more?"

"That you were fuck buddies for a long time until you dumped her."

Rex's face contorted into one of fear. His eyes widened and he stopped breathing for nearly five seconds. "Uh…" He couldn't think of a clever lie to get him out of this rut so he continued to sit there awkwardly, mumbling random words. "Hmm…"

I let him sit on the hot seat a little longer as punishment. "I'm going to be straight with you even though Kayden doesn't want me to. Because I think there's a chance that she means more to you than just some hookup. The reason why she's been sleeping around is because she's heartbroken over you. Before you hooked up, she was in love with you. She's been in love with you for years. She thought if you guys started fooling around, something more serious would happen. When you dumped her, she was devastated. She *still* is devastated."

All the tension left his body once he heard exactly what I said. His eyes found mine, and there was nothing but pure sadness there—along with some self-loathing. "She told you this? She told you she was in love with me?"

"Yes. Under the assumption I wouldn't tell you any of this."

He leaned back into the cushion and stared at the blank TV screen. His features slackened and his eyes were full of nothing but the abyss. He didn't react because he was too shocked by what I just said. "Then why did you tell me?"

"For two reasons. You get to decide which one."

Now he just looked confused.

"If you don't feel anything toward her, then I'm telling you to make you feel like shit. That was really stupid of you, Rex. You shouldn't have fucked around with my best friend and used her like that. She deserves better than that and you know it."

Guilt stretched across his face.

"Or because you might see her as more than just a fuck buddy and you can ask her out on a real date and see where it goes. Now, you decide which reason it's going to be."

Rex didn't say anything for a long time. Seven minutes of pure silence passed while he hardly looked at me. He was stoic like a statue, his thoughts hidden deep behind his eyes. He was normally easy to read, but now he was just an enigma.

"Rex?" I pressed.

"I'm thinking."

"Sorry, I've never seen you think before. Not sure what it looked like." I shouldn't be so vicious right now, but I couldn't help it. I was pissed at him for fooling around with Kayden. It was a miracle they were still friends.

He didn't shoot me a comeback, probably because he was deep in thought. "Does she know about this conversation?"

"No."

"Then why are you telling me?"

"I'm giving you a chance to change things."

"Change things?"

"I've seen you mope around the house for the past month. You haven't been yourself in a long time. I haven't seen you bring a girl over here in that amount of time either, and you seem miserable. It makes me wonder if you're upset over Kayden and you don't even realize it."

He leaned forward and rested his elbows on his knees.

"So?"

"So what?"

"Is that how you feel?"

He pinched the bridge of his nose. "I don't know…"

"How do you not know?" I demanded.

"I just don't, okay? I haven't felt complex emotions like this…ever."

That was dead-on. "If you do decide to pick things up again, don't tell her I told you anything. She made it clear she wanted you to come to her on your own terms, because you want to be with her and no other reason. If she knows I talked to you, she'll think your feelings aren't as sincere."

"Okay."

"You got it?" I asked. "I'm sticking my neck out for you right now, so remember that."

"Why are you doing that?"

"Because I know you, Rex. I know you don't read people very well. I thought giving you a heads up would help you decide what to do. I know you aren't a jerk and would never hurt her on purpose, so you're going to want to make it right—one way or another."

"Well...thanks."

I knew he wouldn't discuss anything else with me so I left the couch.

"So, are you going to make a move on Zeke?" The question came out of nowhere. "I'm sure you know he's single."

I turned back to him. "I'm not gonna pressure him right after he broke up with Rochelle. It would be terrible timing, and I'm sure he's still emotional about the whole thing. When I think he's ready, I'll mention it."

He nodded. "Good call."

Chapter Seventeen

Rex

Rae just dropped a bomb on me, and even days later, I was feeling the aftershocks. Kayden not only felt something more than friendship toward me—but she'd been in love with me for years.

Now when I looked back on the obvious tension between us, I understood what was really going on. She was nervous around me, feeling an attraction that I was totally unaware of. She saw me as something more serious than a friend, and when I picked up girls right in front of her, she was devastated.

Now I knew why she cried that night when we had dinner.

Because I picked up two girls right in front of her.

Damn, I felt like an ass.

How did I not notice how she felt all this time? Every time we had sex, I just thought she was good in bed. I had no clue her feelings extended beyond the mutual pleasure our bodies made when we moved together.

Not a damn clue.

Lately, I'd been bummed about seeing Kayden move on in the dating scene. Every time I saw her, she was with a different guy. And Rae told me she was going through them quicker than anyone else she'd ever known.

But now that I knew the real reason, I understood all the damage I caused.

She was sleeping around so she would stop thinking about me. So her heart would be repaired and she could move on with her life.

This was entirely my fault.

I knew I was jealous when I saw her with other men. When I saw her at the bar with some guy drooling all over her, I was so depressed I went home and straight to bed—at nine. I didn't try picking someone up or calling a regular. All I wanted to do was be alone and suffer in my own misery.

Did that mean I loved her?

Love was a complicated feeling, and I didn't really understand it. I knew I loved Rae because she was my sister and we were family. I knew I loved Zeke because he was my best friend, and he was as good as family. But romantic love…I had no experience in that realm. All I ever felt was my dick get hard—that's it.

If I loved her, I figured I would know. And since I didn't know, I assumed the answer was no.

But I felt something.

I wouldn't be depressed right now if I only saw her as a friend. I wouldn't be jealous of the guys who hit her sheets if she didn't matter to me. I wouldn't hate myself for hurting her if I really didn't give a damn.

There was something there.

Should I tell her?

Should I talk to her?

What would I say?

What would I do?

I wouldn't know until I manned up and did something.

***

When I knocked on her door, I was terrified to see her open it.

What if a guy was in there?

What if I had to watch him walk out, a satisfied smile on his face?

Would I punch him right on the spot?

Kayden cracked the door open. She was in jeans and a t-shirt, probably the clothes she wore to work that day. Her blonde hair was in a braid over one shoulder, and the sunken look in her eyes told me she hadn't slept well in a long time.

Now that I knew how she really felt, I could see the despair burning in her eyes. She was a mess, heartbroken and damaged like a wrecking ball shattered her entire apartment. She was ten pounds lighter than when we started dating, and it was the kind of weight she couldn't afford to lose. She was already so thin as it was.

She cleared her throat before she spoke. "Hey, everything alright?"

No. Nothing was alright. "Yeah...are you busy right now?" If a dude was in there, I'd flip out. I knew it. I couldn't handle it anymore. The jealousy was getting the best of me and turning me into the worst kind of asshole.

"No. What's up?"

"Can I come in?" I still wasn't sure what I would say when I finally had her full attention. It would be so much easier if she could just read my mind and determine what I really wanted.

"Uh, sure." She stepped aside and allowed me into her apartment.

That's when I noticed how baggy her jeans were. They were loose around her hips and waist. I tried not to stare as I walked into her living room and sat down. Right in that spot, she'd ridden me like a cowgirl. Just a few feet over was the place where she sucked me off for the first time. I wondered if any other guy had erased those memories. If they did, I would feel sick.

She sat on the other couch and watched me, clearly awkward with my unexpected visit. "So...what's up?"

I rubbed my palms together and tried to think of something to say. I sorted through different options in my mind but couldn't think of anything good. I decided to go with the truth, the parts that I was certain of. "I hate seeing you with other guys. The other night, when that jackass had his arm around you, I didn't like it."

Kayden's expression finally held some life. She looked astonished, like that was the last thing I could possibly say to her. She was frozen stiff in her seat, completely shocked.

"I know you've been seeing a lot of guys lately because Rae mentioned it and...it bothers me. I haven't been able to sleep well because it's all I can think about. When I picture you with other men, it...hurts." I stared at the floor because I couldn't believe I was saying any of this. "I know I ended our arrangement. At the time, I thought I was fine with it. But I miss you. I miss talking to you. I walked away because I thought I was doing the right thing. I didn't want you to get attached to me. But...I think I got attached to you."

She took a deep breath like she was winded.

I still didn't look at her because I felt awkward saying any of this to her at all. "I'm not sure what I want, Kayden. All I know is, I don't want you to see anyone else. I haven't been with anyone since you, so you don't need to worry about me."

I felt her piercing gaze drill into my face.

I looked up.

The expression she gave me was one I'd never seen before. She was equally stunned and mesmerized at the exact same time. "You haven't been with anyone else?"

I shook my head.

She pointed her finger at her chest. "Just me?"

I nodded. "I haven't had the urge to be with anyone else. When I brought you soup that one day, it was just an excuse to see you. But you threw me out like you didn't want anything to do with me. Then when I saw you with the rest of the gang, you were always hooking up with different guys...and I still didn't want to be with anyone else. I have no idea what I want, but I'm certain of what I don't want."

She wrapped her arms around her tiny torso like she was cold.

"Maybe I'm too late. Maybe you prefer doing what you're doing. But if you're interested...maybe we could go out or something?" I couldn't believe I was asking her out on a date. I'd never done that before, not romantically. My heart was racing in my chest because I was terrified her answer would be no. Maybe she loved me before, but after the way I hurt her, she might not want anything to do with me.

"I'd love that." The emotion caught in her throat and her voice nearly cracked.

"So...no other guys?" I wasn't usually the monogamous type, but I wanted to know I would be the only man in her life right now.

"No other guys," she whispered.

I immediately felt better. All the weight I'd been carrying on my shoulders finally disappeared. The stress on my chest was gone, and I finally found some peace. I stared at her on the other couch and felt my longing grow. I hadn't had any alone time with her in over a month. And now she was just a few feet away.

I moved to the couch beside her and wrapped my arm around her waist. Just like before, it felt right. It seemed like her waist was made just for my arm. I pulled her close to me and rested my face against hers. "I don't care if anyone knows about us." I had to pretend I didn't know Rae knew, and I felt deceitful for saying it. But Zeke didn't know, and I needed to tell him before Rae beat me to the punch. "If they give us shit for it, then whatever."

She finally smiled, a beautiful one. The depressed features of her face suddenly softened, fading away as her happiness shone through. The look she gave me was one I'd seen a hundred times but never really noticed. But this time, I noticed.

And I would always notice.

Chapter Eighteen

Rae

"That guy is totally checking you out." I noticed him glance at Jessie a few times before his glances turned into full-blown staring. He could barely keep his eyes off her for more than a few minutes. He was her type with dark skin, dark hair, and mocha-colored eyes.

Jessie played it cool as she stood beside me at the bar. "Where?"

"Three o'clock."

"Tell me when he's not looking." She sipped her third drink.

I was already on my fourth. "Okay, now."

She quickly glanced, looked him up and down, and then faced forward again. She did it all in stride and with perfect grace. "I like what I see."

My buzz was quickly turning into a drunken haze. I could feel the fog cover my eyes and lower my inhibitions. "You gonna go for it?"

"No. I'm gonna play it cool for a little bit."

I didn't question her game. She knew what she was doing.

"See anyone you like?"

I didn't bother looking around. "Zeke isn't here. So no, I don't see anyone I like."

"Girl, pick up a guy for the night. Who knows how long it will be before Zeke is ready to move forward. You should get some while you wait. You've waited long enough as it is."

I hadn't gotten laid in four months, and the dry spell was killing me. "It doesn't matter how horny I am. The only person I want is Zeke. This room could be full of Chippendales, and I still wouldn't feel anything."

"Damn, you've got it bad."

"I know." I sighed and slouched at the counter. "He's so hot, Jessie. Like, you don't understand."

"I have eyes," she snapped. "Yes, I understand."

"I just want to grab his face and kiss him. I want to ride him all night long. How did I not notice just how damn perfect he was?"

She shrugged. "Beats me." She downed the rest of her drink before she turned to me. "I'm going to make my move. I have a feeling I'm not gonna come back. You'll make it home on your own okay?"

I rolled my eyes. "I'm a big girl. Don't worry about me."

"You're sure? You're on the road to Hammerville."

"I know how to use a phone. Seriously, go. Have an orgasm for me."

"On it." She kissed me on the cheek before she walked away. She strutted up to her prey, flashed a smile, and he was hers.

I sat at the bar and ordered another drink. I stuck out like a sore thumb sitting alone, but I didn't care. I was happy that Jessie landed a stud for the

357

evening. The only stud I wanted was probably at home playing video games.

"Hey, I'm Paul." Some guy appeared out of nowhere and extended his hand.

I shook it. "Hi, Paul. I'm Rae."

"Pretty name for a pretty girl."

What a line.

"Can I get you another drink?"

"No." I raised my hand. "I've already had one too many."

"Then can I sit here and watch you drink it?"

He seemed like a nice guy, and I felt bad for blowing him off. "I'll be honest with you. I'm hung up on some other guy right now. Not looking for anything."

"Then why aren't you with him?"

"He doesn't know I exist..."

"Well, how about I help you get over him? You can get under me, and by morning, he'll be out of your head."

And another line. "I appreciate the offer, but I'm not interested. But thanks for talking to me."

"Well, I'll see you around, Rae."

"You too, Paul."

He walked away, and I stared at my drink in misery. I felt the alcohol seep further into my body and confuse me even more. I couldn't differentiate time and my lids were falling. When I looked for Jessie, I couldn't find her. But then again, I couldn't remember what she looked like.

I knew I needed to get out of there before I did something really stupid. So I walked outside and did something stupid anyway. I called Zeke.

He answered after a few rings. "Hey, pizza girl."

I didn't care about the nickname. "Here's the deal..." I could barely put my words together. "I'm totally drunk right now at this place...and I don't know where I am. So—"

"I'm on my way. What bar are you at?"

I turned around and squinted at the sign. "Voodoodoodoo…"

"Voodoo?" he asked with a chuckle.

"I don't know…there's a lot of O's."

"I'll be there as soon as possible. Are you standing outside?"

"Yep. I'm wearing a tiny little dress like a hooker."

He chuckled again. "I love it when you're drunk."

"So you can take advantage of me?" I asked hopefully. I'd give anything to feel his lips all over my body.

"I wish. But I'm too much of a good guy."

I couldn't tell if he was kidding or not.

"Hold tight. I'll be there soon."

***

Zeke pulled up in his Jeep and opened his driver door.

"I got it." I opened the passenger door but nearly fell into the gutter.

Zeke showed mercy by not laughing. He gripped me by the hips and hoisted me inside like I weighed nothing. He protected my head then scooted my legs across the seat. He even went the extra mile and buckled my safety belt.

"I'm not a child."

"But you walk like Bambi. So you're worse than a child." He smiled before he shut the door.

He got on the road and pushed through the traffic of the night. He didn't ask me any questions about my night.

I knew he was taking me home, but I didn't want to go there. "Could we go to your place?"

"Why?" He kept his eyes on the road.

"I just don't want to deal with Rex. He usually pulls pranks when I'm drunk."

"Like the time he poured melted butter all over you while you were sleeping?"

I'd never forget how sticky my hair was when I woke up in the morning. "Yes..."

He laughed. "That was pretty good, you have to admit that."

I shot him a glare.

"Alright." He turned on his blinker. "We'll go to my place until you sober up."

He drove to his place near the coast and on a secluded road. His front yard was covered with trees and grass, and the porch light was on. He pulled into the garage and shut the door behind him before he helped me into the house.

"Want some tea?" he asked. "It usually helps me when I'm wasted. A little honey helps it go down easier too."

"No, it's okay." I leaned against the wall and pulled off my heels. All the little straps made it nearly impossible. All I did was tug and nearly snapped my ankle.

Zeke spotted my discomfort then kneeled down to help me. He held my leg and balanced me as he pulled one heel off. Then he undid the other before he slipped it off my foot. He touched my body delicately despite the strong muscles that covered his body. Then he rose to his full height and looked at me, his blue eyes suddenly intense.

I knew I wasn't myself, and I needed to be as logical as possible. But, I didn't want to be logical. I'd spent all night at a bar, but all I could do was think about him. I didn't want to sleep in my own bed with a massive dog. I wanted to share my bed with him.

My eyes moved to his lips and the urge took over. I wanted my hands all over him, and I wanted those strong hands all over me. My inhibitions were so low they were practically non-existent, and right now, it didn't seem like a bad idea to kiss him.

So I did.

I wrapped my arms around his neck and pressed my mouth to his like I'd done it a hundred times. My lips brushed against his before they fully came together. They were soft and full like I expected, and the second we connected, I felt the chemistry I'd been dreaming about. Reality was difficult to understand when I was floating like this. Like I was on a cloud, I felt higher than the sky.

My hands cupped his neck, and I felt his powerful pulse underneath my touch. Even his neck was corded and muscular. I could feel the strength in every inch of his physique. My hands slid down to his shoulders, and I felt their solid strength.

But nothing compared to how good his mouth felt on mine.

Zeke kissed me back slowly, like he'd been expecting the embrace to happen. The kiss was restrained, like he was holding himself back from doing what he really wanted. But then his resistance snapped, and he cupped my face with his warm hand and pressed me against the wall. He kissed me harder once he had me pinned, his muscled chest pressed right against mine. He breathed hard into my mouth then gave me some of his tongue, taking the kiss to a level I'd wanted for weeks.

I wanted him between my legs then and there. I wanted to undo his jeans so he could take me right in the entryway. I'd been waiting so long to have this gorgeous man, and I didn't want to wait any longer. It didn't matter how stupid of an idea this was. My impatience got the best of me.

But Zeke ended it.

He pulled away then cleared his throat, the regret and desire battling in his eyes. He stepped back and cleared his throat.

I felt the cold rejection sweep across me. That kiss was fantastic, even if I was drunk, and I didn't want it to end. I didn't want Zeke to push me away just because he saw me as a friend. If he ever gave me another chance, I could make him see me in a different way.

"I'm gonna make that tea..." He walked into the kitchen.

I wanted to slide to the floor and never get up again. But the tile was cold, and I was in a short dress. I went into the living room and lay on the couch, wanting to fall asleep and forget this night ever happened. I shouldn't have called Zeke in the first place.

The one good thing about this situation was I probably wouldn't remember it in the morning.

Thank god.

I closed my eyes for a moment, and must have drifted off, because Zeke's appearance startled me.

He set the tea on the table, steam billowing from the surface. He eyed me with concern before he sat on the edge of the table and watched me.

I tried to sit up, but I was too weak. "I'm sorry..."

"It's okay, Rae."

"I'm just really drunk right now..."

"You don't need to explain. It's not a big deal."

"It is a big deal." That kiss wasn't just sexually motivated. There was a lot more to it.

"I can forget about if it if you can."

He was giving me a way out because he was a good guy. But I didn't want a good guy. "I don't want to forget about it…"

His eyes softened.

I scooted against the back of the couch then patted the cushion beside me. "Lie with me."

He considered the suggestion before he slipped off his shoes and got comfortable beside me.

My arm immediately went around his neck and I hooked my leg around his waist, doing exactly what I wanted despite the way he stopped our kiss.

He didn't push me off him. Instead, he grabbed the blanket hanging over the back of the couch and covered us with it, hiding the bottom half of our bodies from view. Then he wrapped his arm around my waist and pulled me closer to him, his face just inches from mine.

It was heaven.

And maybe even better than that kiss.

I'd fantasized about a moment like this at work. I pictured us lying together on the couch with the TV on in the background, rain hitting the patio door as it sprinkled. I pictured Safari lying on the floor with his eyes closed. This was what I wanted every single day.

When he shifted his position, I could feel the definition of his cock through his jeans right against my hips. It was thick, long, and large. Exactly what I hoped was hiding inside those jeans. He must have known it was there because it was too big to ignore.

Which meant he wanted me.

He was still attracted to me.

There was hope.

"Zeke, you're so hot." I never would have blurted that out in a million years without drinking three Long Island Iced Tea and two lemons drops.

His deep voice came out quietly. "I think you're hot too, Rae."

"But I think you're really hot. Like, damn."

He smiled with his eyes and not his lips. "I thought about you in the shower this morning. Can you top that?"

My pussy immediately clenched. "Yes, I can. Because I think about you every night."

The heat came into his gaze and he squeezed me a little tighter. He pressed his face against mine but didn't kiss me. "What are you doing to me?"

"Not nearly enough."

He brushed his lips across my cheek before he placed a kiss on my forehead. "Close your eyes and get some sleep."

The last thing I wanted to do was get some sleep. "I'm not normally like this..."

He stared at me, not understanding my meaning.

"I don't throw myself at guys like this. When I went to the bar with Jessie, all I could think about was you. I've never wanted someone I couldn't have so badly."

His hand moved through my hair slowly, and it looked like he might kiss me again. "You can have me, Rae. Just not tonight."

"Why?"

"Because you aren't going to remember this in the morning."

***

I woke up with the worst migraine ever.

Luckily, two pills were sitting on the table with a glass of water. I tossed them down my throat and practically chugged the water. I sat upright and felt the pain in my head increase with every movement.

Damn, what happened last night?

Zeke walked over with a plate in his hand. He set it on the table, and that's when I saw the veggie omelet. "You had a rough night."

"Yeah...I kinda figured." I pulled the plate toward me. "Thanks for breakfast. That was nice of you."

"Of course." He sat beside me and kept staring at me.

"What?" I asked without taking my eyes off my food.

"How do you feel?"

"I've been better."

He kept staring at me. "Do you remember anything about last night?"

"Why? Did I do something stupid?" I ate half of the omelet before I looked at him.

He held my gaze. "No. You called me and asked for a ride. Wasn't sure if you remembered that."

"Actually, no. But I figured that's what happened when I woke up on your couch."

He leaned back into the couch and waited for me to finish my breakfast.

"Sorry, I crashed on your couch last night."

"It's no big deal. You know my couch always has your name written on it."

"Thanks," I said with a smile. I finished my breakfast and wiped the plate clean. "I'll get out of your hair and take an Uber home." I placed my dish in the sink then grabbed my shoes from the corner.

"I don't mind taking you home." Zeke followed me, wearing his sweatpants and a Mariners t-shirt.

"It's okay. You've done enough." I wanted to hug him goodbye but I suddenly felt awkward doing that. I already called him to pick me up last night. My feelings for Zeke were obviously directing most of my behavior.

"Are you sure? I really don't mind."

"It's okay. I'll probably go to Jessie's so I can hear about her night. I'll see you later."

This time, he didn't fight me. "Alright. Lunch tomorrow?"

My workday was so much better when I met him for lunch. "Yeah, sure."

"I'll text you where."

"Alright. Bye."

"Bye." He watched me go before he shut the door.

Ray of Love

Chapter Nineteen

Rex

Zeke slid into the booth across from me and ordered a beer from the bartender. Wings were already on the table so he grabbed a few and munched on them like everything was perfectly normal.

"So...Rae slept over last night?" I kept the accusation out of my tone, but only by sheer determination. When Rae said she crashed at his place, I wasn't allowed to ask any questions, based on my agreement with her. But I was sure as hell gonna ask Zeke about it.

"Yeah." He grabbed a few more wings and kept eating.

"That's it? You aren't going to elaborate on that?"

With a straight face, he stopped eating and said, "I will when you tell me about Kayden."

I shut my mouth immediately.

Now his look was full of accusation. "Yeah, Rae told me. Not you, Rae."

"Let me explain—"

"Yeah, you better get on that."

I told him everything from the beginning until the present point in time.

He gave me the same lifeless expression. "And you thought that was a good idea?"

"She offered herself to me. Was I supposed to say no?"

"Yes, idiot."

"Like you would say no if Rae offered herself to you."

"I did last night," he snapped.

Now all my thoughts of Kayden were gone. "Whoa, let's back up... What happened?"

"She came on to me a few times last night. She was pretty drunk, and she's usually aggressive when she's drunk. She kissed me and I stopped it. That's really about it."

I slammed my hands down on the table. "That's it? You just had your first kiss with Rae."

"No, I didn't."

"So you've kissed her before?" My nostrils flared.

"No." He spoke in a bored voice. "It doesn't count."

"It sure as hell does count."

"Not when she doesn't remember it."

"Oh...she woke up this morning and forgot?"

He nodded. "She was totally hammered, man. I wasn't going to start anything up when she was like that. Don't get me wrong, I was flattered. Never in my wildest dreams did I expect Rae to—" He stopped talking when he saw the pissed look on my face. "I just didn't think we should start off like that. Since she wouldn't remember any of it, that made it easier. We can keep doing what we're doing, and when I'm ready, I'll go for it."

"And when is that going to be?"

"Soon." That was all he said.

"Rochelle has been gone for almost a month now. I think you've waited long enough."

"Yeah, I think I have too. But I want the moment to be right, you know?"

"I'm sure Rae is waiting for the same moment."

"Yeah, you're probably right," he said.

"So funny," I said. "You both have feelings for each other, but you guys don't know it."

"I know she has feelings for me," he corrected.

"Yeah, but she's clueless about your feelings for her."

"And let's keep it that way," he said. "You didn't tell her, right?"

"Nope." I zipped my lips. "Which is why you should forgive me for the whole Kayden thing."

He glared at me. "You lied to me for six months. You're going to have to step it up if you want forgiveness."

"Oh, come on. It was a complicated situation."

"You still could have told me no matter how complicated it was. And what's going on now? Are you dating?" He grabbed a handful of fries and shoved them onto his plate. He grabbed the bottle of ketchup and squirted it across.

"I asked her if she wanted to have dinner. I wouldn't say we're dating. We're just not seeing other people."

Zeke gave me a look I'd been getting from him my whole life. "That means you're dating."

"No, not really. We're just hanging out exclusively."

"Dating."

"Hell no. We aren't fooling around."

"You aren't?" he asked in surprise.

"No. I want to take a different approach this time."

Now he smirked. "So, dating."

"Shut the hell up, man."

"I'm just telling you how it is. Not my fault if you don't want to see it that way."

When I thought about his definition of dating, I realized I could use it against him. "Then you and Rae are dating."

"How so?"

"You're not seeing anyone but each other. You have feelings for each other but you don't fool around. Boom! You're dating."

He considered my words as he munched on a handful of fries. "I guess you aren't dating Kayden."

"Take that, asshole."

"But does it really count if she doesn't know?" he questioned. "Because she doesn't know how I feel about her yet. So...I think you're wrong."

He had me and I knew it. "Damn..."

"Sorry, man. Better luck next time."

***

I arrived at Kayden's door with a handful of flowers. I saw them in the store window when I walked to her apartment, so I thought I would grab a few to make a good impression. I pissed all over my other first impression.

When she opened the door, her mouth formed the biggest smile I'd ever seen. "Oh, wow. They're beautiful." She took them from my hands and immediately smelled them. "Thanks so much..."

Seeing how happy the simple gesture made her somehow made me feel like shit. I could have treated her better to begin with if I just put in a little effort. Instead, I was an asshole and stomped all over her heart. "You're welcome. Are you ready for dinner?"

"Yeah." She put the flowers in a vase filled with water then grabbed her clutch. She wore leggings with a long blouse on top. It flattered her beautiful curves, and the color complemented her nice skin tone as well. She looked perfect, like always.

I knew I should tell her that. "You look...really... yeah." That was the best I could do. I was nervous because I'd never done this before, and I was already in the dog house for screwing everything up to begin with.

She understood it was the best I could do. "Thanks. You look handsome, like always."

She said it so why couldn't I? "Thanks."

We went to an Italian café a few blocks from her apartment. It was nice but not too fancy. I didn't want our first date to be too intense since I was already uncomfortable as it was. The pressure was on my shoulders, and she probably felt the strain as well.

She looked at her menu, her gaze down and her eyes scanning as she read the selections.

I didn't have an appetite so I just picked the first thing on the list.

After the waiter came and took our orders, he disappeared and left us alone together.

She used to be the awkward one when we were alone together, but now I was the awkward one. "How was work?"

"Good. But I think I'm going to be leaving soon."

"Why?"

"The director said they're closing down the library later this year. Not enough income to keep the lights on. People just don't go to the library anymore. Everything is digital now."

"Wow, I'm so sorry."

She shrugged. "It's okay. I'll find another job. I have a lot of time to get everything together."

"I still feel bad. I know you love that place."

"Well, I love being surrounded by books all day. But, I can always do that when I get home."

I wanted to say something to make her feel better, but I couldn't think of anything.

"How's Groovy Bowl?"

"Good," I answered. "Things have been going well since we reopened a few months ago. I used to think it was just a grand opening rush, but now I think it's the norm."

"That's great, Rex." She gave me that smile that said she was proud of me.

I liked that smile.

"Thanks. I'm really glad Zeke and Rae helped me out. I wouldn't be here without them."

"They're great friends. No doubt about that."

When I considered her situation at the library, an idea came to me. "Why don't you open your own bookstore? You know, a bookstore and a coffee shop. There are a lot of college kids around here that could use the Wi-Fi and a coffee."

"Oh, I don't know about that. I'm not really a businesswoman."

"I'm not a businessman either," I said. "It's not as hard as it sounds."

She shrugged. "I don't really want to work with customers and make coffee. I really only care about the books."

"You could hire people to do those other things. You would just oversee the store, organize book signings, decorate, decide what books will get on the shelves, stuff like that. It doesn't have to be enormous, just a small shop."

"No matter how small it is, it still sounds ambitious to me."

"Give yourself more credit, Kayden." When she put her mind to something, she always succeeded. She wasn't the most confident person, but that didn't mean she wasn't competent. "I have no doubt you could do it and do an awesome job."

She shrugged modestly. "I'll think about it. I'll have to figure something out soon..."

An idea popped into my mind, and it was kind of a crazy one. "What if you work for me?"

"At Groovy Bowl?" she asked with a small laugh.

"Why not?" I asked. "You could be a manager and oversee things. Plus, you and I could make out in the office..." I waggled my eyebrows.

She laughed harder. "I don't know the first thing about bowling."

"Like I do. And it could be temporary until you figure out what you really want to do."

"True. Well, thanks for the offer."

"Of course. But I do expect you to go above and beyond...if you know what I mean."

She rolled her eyes. "Of course I do, Rex. Wouldn't expect anything less."

***

After dinner, we got ice cream then I walked her home. The beginning of the night was awkward because of everything we'd been through. I kept picturing all the guys she brought back to her place, even though I didn't want to. None of that would have happened if I'd pulled my head out of my ass sooner.

I was surprised how much fun we had considering we'd known each other for so long. I felt like I got to know her all over again, but in a different way. She was still tense around me, but by the end of the night, she was relaxed and herself.

I couldn't remember the last time I had that much fun.

I walked her to her door and felt my cock harden inside my jeans. Spending the evening with her made me want to finish off the night with something unforgettable. But a different version of myself held me back. I asked her out because I wanted something more than a physical relationship. If I wanted to do things the right way, we had to slow down. "Thanks for going out with me."

"Thanks for taking me..." She stared at me like she expected me to kiss her.

I wanted to hold her but I thought even that was too sexual. "I'd like to go out again." I didn't want her to think I wasn't going to call. I was there for the long haul. But I was also doing everything as slowly as possible.

"Me too."

"I'll call you tomorrow."

She couldn't hide her surprise at the odd dismissal of our date. "Do you want to come inside?"

More than anything in the goddamn world. "I want things to be different this time."

She nodded like she understood.

"I don't just want to just hook up. I want more."

"I do too."

"So...let's take it slow."

"Okay."

A kiss shouldn't be too intense, right? I wrapped my arms around her waist and immediately felt the comfort of the familiar intimacy. She had womanly hips and a beautifully narrow waist. She felt a little different in my embrace because of the weight she lost, but she was still perfect.

I pressed my forehead against hers and just held her, forgetting the kiss because the embrace was just as good. I closed my eyes as I felt her heartbeat pound against my chest. It was wild and out of control, her emotions all over the place.

I pulled her closer into me, feeling my breathing increase as the longing overtook me. I took our relationship for granted once before, but I would never do that again. It wasn't until I lost Kayden that I realized I had the love of a remarkable woman. I was too stupid to realize it then, but I definitely realized it now.

"I missed this..." Her words disappeared into the fabric of my shirt.

My arms tightened around her waist, and I rested my chin on her head. Together, we stood alone in the hallway with our arms wrapped around one another. It felt good just to stand there and hold her, ignoring the passing of time. "I missed this too."

Ray of Love

Chapter Twenty

Rae

I put on the dress Jessie let me borrow, the black heels that went with it, and I went a little extreme on my hair. I'd never spent much time getting ready for anything, but tonight, I went all out. I curled my hair and sprayed the shit out of them so they would stay in all night—and hopefully last until the morning.

I was sick of waiting to make my move on Zeke.

Absolutely sick of it.

I seriously had the hots for him, and this obsession was only getting worse. When I had lunch with him yesterday, I wanted to jump across the table and straddle his hips like I owned him. When I slept at his place, I wanted to wake up naked in his enormous bed.

I couldn't keep these feelings in any longer.

If he rejected me, ouch. But if he didn't...I might go home with him tonight.

391

"Damn, you look hot." Jessie walked into my bedroom and looked me up and down with approval. "I knew that would fit you perfectly. Your tits look awesome and your legs go on for days."

A comment like that would be strange if it came from anyone besides Jessie or Kayden. But since they were my best friends, they could say anything they wanted and get away with it. "Thanks."

"I'm guessing you're going for it tonight?" She sat on my bed and watched me get ready in the mirror on my vanity.

"Yep." I applied a layer of lip gloss and fixed my hair. "For better or worse."

"Well, he's gonna have a hard time turning you down, that's for sure."

Kayden knocked before she walked in. "Hey—" Her mouth stretched into an enormous smile. "Damn, Rae's got her groove back."

"You like?" I turned and posed for her.

"Yeah. But you know who's really going to like it?" Kayden said. "That hunk, Zeke."

"God, I hope so." After one more look in the mirror, I turned away. "Alright, any changes?"

Jessie looked me up and down then shook her head. "You look perfect."

"More than perfect," Kayden said. "The only way Zeke isn't going to want you is if he's gay."

"I'm pretty sure he's not," I said. "So my odds are good."

"Then let's get going." Jessie grabbed my perfume then sprayed it up my dress.

"Uh, excuse me?" I swatted her hand away.

"You gotta make sure you smell good everywhere," Jessie reminded me. "I mean, it's been four months of neglect down there. Who knows what's happened in that time of isolation."

"She's fine," I said. "But thanks for checking."

"Did you shave?" Kayden asked.

"Even better," I said. "I got waxed this morning—from head to toe."

Jessie gave me a thumbs-up. "Let's go get you some action. Because if Zeke turns you down, we're gonna make sure you get laid anyway."

***

When we arrived at the bar, Zeke and Rex were already there. They stood at one of the high-top tables with their beers on coasters. The game was on the TVs so their eyes were glued to the screens most of the time.

"Rae, you go first so Zeke can see you the best." Jessie gave me a gentle nudge.

"Strut it," Kayden said. "And hard."

"I know how to walk, guys," I hissed.

"Well, walk sexy," Jessie said.

"Okay, I don't quite know how to do that," I said. "But I can try." I walked to the front and approached the table with my clutch tucked under my arm.

When Zeke saw me approach in his periphery, he turned to stare at me head on. Instead of flashing me his typical smile, his eyes darkened with considerable heat. Freely, his eyes roamed over my body, moving from my dark eyeliner and painted lips, all the way down my short dress to my black stilettos.

Speechless, he just stared.

I think I nailed it.

Rex stared at me with indifference, like usual. Then his eyes moved to Kayden, and he gave her a look identical to the one Zeke just gave me. He whistled under his breath. "Damn, woman. Are you trying to give me a heart attack?"

"A heart attack?" Kayden asked.

"Yeah," Rex said. "You know, because most of my blood has drained elsewhere."

I was too busy staring at Zeke to care about what my brother just said. Zeke liked the way I looked in the dress, but I liked the way he looked even more. He wore a dark green t-shirt that fit tightly over his pectoral muscles. I could see the definition of his arms through the fabric. His corded forearms led to strong hands, the kind I wanted all over my body. His black jeans hung low on his hips, and I couldn't help but picture those V lines that extended above his waistband.

The fact that he didn't even try to look sexy just made him sexier. He didn't do his hair. When he walked out of the shower, he dried it with a towel and that was the end of it. He was sexy enough to be on a firemen calendar, but he didn't possess the arrogance of someone that good-looking.

Damn, he was perfect.

Zeke continued to stare at me, not saying hi like he normally would.

I didn't say anything either. Words left me.

The rest of the gang talked like normal.

Rex wrapped his arm around Kayden's waist. "I know this is weird for all of us. But yes, Kayden and I are seeing each other. We understand the risks it could pose to our friendship and the group. But we both want this, and we hope you guys can accept it."

My eyes never left Zeke's.

He didn't turn away either. "Whatever you want, man."

"Are you going to even look at us?" Rex demanded.

I sighed before I turned to my brother. "Congrats. You have a girlfriend. Good for you."

"Whoa, I didn't say anything about a girlfriend." Rex dropped his hand. "We're just seeing each other."

"Exclusively," Zeke jabbed. "She's your girlfriend. Just admit it."

"He's right," Kayden said. "I'm your girlfriend, and I better be addressed as such."

Rex didn't have a rebuttal when those words left her lips. "Alright, cool."

Jessie laughed. "Pussy-whipped already."

"I'm so not pussy-whipped," Rex snapped.

"You are, man," Zeke said. "But you know what? That's okay. Guys are the happiest when they are pussy-whipped."

"Really?" Rex asked in surprise.

"Oh yeah." Zeke nodded before he looked at me. "Can I get you a drink?"

Butterflies flew across my stomach. "Sure. A lemon drop."

"Be right back." He left his beer on the table before he headed to the bar on the other side of the room.

Jessie smirked at me once he was out of earshot. "Drooling all over you, dude."

"Yeah?" When I smiled, I felt the blush enter my cheeks.

"He was speechless when you walked up to him," Jessie said. "Didn't have a clue what to say."

Kayden and Rex were absorbed in their own conversation, quietly whispering together.

"He was quiet, wasn't he?" I said.

"Because all the blood left his body and went into that huge dick of his," Jessie said. "He probably couldn't even think."

I spotted him coming back with my drink in hand. "Shh...be cool."

"Oh, come on," Jessie said. "Like Zeke doesn't know he has a big dick."

"How do you know?" I asked.

She shrugged. "Look at the guy. Sometimes you can just tell."

"You'll have to teach me that little gift of yours when we have some downtime."

"Ha," she said. "I'll take my secrets to the grave."

Zeke returned to the table and placed the lemon drop beside me. "Here you go. I got you one too, Jess." He slid the drink to her side of the table.

"Awe, thanks." Jessie grabbed the glass by the stem and took a big drink. "Always so nice."

"What about Kayden?" Rex demanded. "You didn't bring her anything?"

Zeke gave him a hard stare. "I think her *boyfriend* should be the one to fetch her a drink."

"Oh shit," Rex said under his breath. "I didn't even think of that."

Zeke nodded to the bar like he was giving some kind of code.

Rex understood his meaning. "Oh yeah. What would you like?"

"I'll take a lemon drop too," Kayden said. "And thank you."

"Be right back." Rex gave her a thumbs-up before he walked to the bar.

Zeke's eyes never left my face now that there were no more distractions. The look he gave me was different than the others. It was full of intensity—even desperation.

Or perhaps it was just wishful thinking on my part.

"You look amazing." His eyes moved down to my thighs, just where the dress ended inches above my knee.

"Thanks. You do too."

"I don't think we're on the same level, but thanks."

I sipped my drink just so I had something to do. He suddenly made me nervous, hot and cold all over. All I could do was picture my mouth devouring his, sucking that bottom lip into my mouth before I grazed his tongue with my own. I wanted that handsome body on top of mine in the darkness of his bedroom, the headboard tapping against the wall as he nailed me like a sailor home on leave.

Now I really needed to make a move. There was no way I was going home without him.

I just had to decide how to do that.

***

The guys walked to the corner to watch the end of the game. The score was tied and it was the final inning of overtime. Most of the guys in the bar were crowded around the TVs, needing to see the final outcome of the cutthroat game.

"Are you going to do it?" Kayden asked.

"Oh yeah," I said. "Just not sure how I should go for it."

"Just tell him you want to go back to his place," Jessie said. "And ta-da. You win."

"Since Zeke is my friend, it's more complicated than that." I couldn't just hook up with him without some kind of explanation. "I was thinking I could tell him I've been into him for a few months now and I'd like to make a move. And if he's into that...I'll do it."

"Too much talking," Kayden said.

"I agree," Jessie said. "Romance is so much better when people shut up."

"Well, it would be really awkward if I just kissed him and he wasn't into me at all." Doing something stupid could affect our friendship, something I held very close to my heart.

"Shut up," Jessie said. "He was drooling all over you."

"He so was," Kayden said. "Didn't even try to hide it."

"Still...I shouldn't make an assumption." Now I was just looking for an excuse because I was nervous to actually do it. I'd hit on guys before and had no problem making the first move, but this was the first guy who really mattered. He wasn't just some hot dude. He was the hottest, sweetest, and most amazing dude on the planet.

"So when he comes back over here, go for it," Jessie said. "Kayden and I will go to the bar or something to give you some privacy."

I downed the rest of my glass. "Alright. Let's do this." I turned back to the corner where Zeke and Rex were standing. Some brunette was standing close to Zeke and chatting his ear off. She wore a skin-tight blue dress, and she was definitely a looker.

"Doesn't mean anything." Jessie could read me like a book.

But they kept talking. And Zeke even laughed at something she said. The game was over, but he still stayed to talk to her.

I was getting nervous. Did I just miss my chance?

"Still doesn't mean anything," Kayden said. "He's just being nice."

"You guys, let's not pretend she's not gorgeous," I snapped. "He's not just being nice to her."

She and Zeke stepped away from the crowd and kept talking. His body faced my direction but he didn't look up to see me. He held his beer in his hand and continued to listen to her talk. It didn't seem like he was coming back.

"Fuck, why does this always happen to me?" I gripped the table for support. "I don't want him when I can have him, but now that I can actually have him, he doesn't want me."

"We still don't know—" Jessie stopped talking when she saw the woman grip Zeke's bicep. "Okay...maybe you're right."

I wasn't just upset because I was jealous. I was upset I didn't do something sooner when I had the chance. Instead of waiting to make sure Zeke had enough time to move on from Rochelle, I should have just gone for it.

Now I was full of regret.

"Excuse me." Just as I left the table, Zeke looked up at me. His eyes bored straight into mine as the woman continued to press her luscious body up against him. I pretended I didn't give a damn and headed into the hallway where the bathrooms were located.

To my misfortune, there was a line of women against the wall waiting to use the bathroom. I couldn't go back out there, so I leaned against the wall near the men's room, attempting some privacy away from everyone else. And then I tried to talk myself down from the sheer terror in my heart.

You have no right to be jealous.

It'll be alright.

There are other fish in the sea.

No, there're no other fish in the sea. He's it.

God, did I just lose the greatest thing that could have ever happened to me?

I wanted him so much.

I felt tears prickle my eyes. They were warm, and the bubbling sensation in the corners of my eyes just made me feel worse. I cried when Ryker dumped me because I was heartbroken. But I'd never cried over a man I didn't have. That only convinced me my feelings for Zeke were stronger than anything I'd ever felt in my life.

And that just made me feel worse.

And fucking hopeless.

I took a deep breath and stilled my tears. I had to go back out there and pretend everything was fine.

If I let these tears fall, my eyes would turn bloodshot red and puffy. It would be a dead giveaway that something was wrong.

Just when I wiped my fingers under my eyes to fix my makeup, Zeke walked into the hallway. He scanned the area like he was looking for someone. Then his eyes settled on me, his target.

A breath of time passed between us. I prayed he didn't notice the puffiness surrounding my eyes. I hoped he didn't see just how heartbroken I was when some woman touched him. It was obvious I was head over heels for him. I just hoped it wasn't obvious to him.

He slowly walked toward me, taking his time despite the determination in his eyes. He moved right up to me, pressing me harder against the solid surface of the wall. His chest moved against mine and our mouths were just inches apart.

I didn't know what was happening. But I think I liked it.

He grabbed both of my hands, interlocked our fingers, and pinned them against the wall as he moved closer to me.

Now I couldn't breathe.

He brushed his lips against mine, practically teasing me. It was the calm before the storm, the pause before the fall. He brushed his lips past mine again before he finally dove in and kissed me hard on the mouth.

Oh god.

He sucked my bottom lip before he moved his entire mouth with mine. Every kiss was purposeful, magical. He breathed hard into my mouth with an intensity that matched my own. His chest rose and fell with every deep breath, and a quiet moan escaped his lips when he felt my mouth with his.

I fought against his hold because I wanted to touch him, to run my hands all over that muscled physique. But he wouldn't let me move. He pinned me harder into the wall, keeping me in place as he deepened his kiss.

I was his prisoner. His property. His girl.

And I knew it.

His fingers tightened around mine and he kissed me in that dark hallway, not caring about the people in line or the men who walked out of the bathroom and headed to the bar. His hips pressed against mine and his enormous definition rubbed against me through his jeans.

Was this a dream?

He kissed me forever, never slowing down or stopping his intensity. He was rough with my lips, making me feel like I'd never kissed anyone before. Everything about our embrace was unique—perfect.

He finally broke apart and pressed his face to mine. "Rae, I'm yours. And you've always been mine."

***

As soon as he shut the front door, his lips were on mine again. He kissed me just as hard as he did before, and this time, he scooped me up by the ass and pulled me against his waist. He carried me down the hall and into his bedroom.

I'd never been inside it before but I didn't care about looking around. All the lights were off, and my back hit his soft bedding when he laid me down.

He immediately pulled his shirt over his chest and tossed it on the floor.

Oh my lord.

So perfect.

Mine. All mine.

Perfectly chiseled and beautiful, every time he moved, his muscles rippled in response. He was lean and toned—practically ripped. He grabbed one ankle and removed my heel in one fluid motion. Then he did the same to the other. When my feet were bare, he placed one foot against his chest then leaned down and kissed me on the ankle.

"Ooh…" I didn't consider my ankle to be an erogenous zone, but he sure made it into one.

He did the same with the other and pressed both feet against his massive chest. His heart beat against my heel, strong and powerful.

I dug my toes into his skin, feeling the searing heat that kept me warm. He was so goddamn hot that I couldn't even wrap my mind around it. My pussy was already drenched, and I wanted that enormous package inside me—as soon as possible.

With my feet still pressed to his chest, he undid his jeans and dropped them to his ankles. He kicked his shoes and socks away, and then kicked off his black pants. He was just in his boxers, solid black and dark in comparison to his fair and flawless skin. He grabbed the waistband of his boxers and felt the fabric with his fingertips, his blue eyes watching my face the entire time.

Drop em'.

Come on, drop em'.

He pulled them down his muscular thighs, his enormous cock popping out proudly.

I bit my bottom lip. "Oh wow…"

He pulled them off and stood in his glorious nakedness. His natural lubrication was oozing from the tip, glistening as he stared at me on his bed.

I'd never felt so happy to be alive.

His hands glided up my thighs until he reached my hips. He bunched up the fabric of my dress then pulled it up to my waist, exposing my belly button. My feet were still planted firmly against his chest.

His fingers found the fabric of my thong. He fisted each strap tightly before he yanked it down my thighs and to my knees. He let it hang there because my feet were still braced against him. His hand moved back down to my ass and gripped it harshly, dragging me toward the edge of the bed. "Mine." He kneeled to the floor and moved my legs over his shoulders, my panties still stretched between my knees. His face moved between my legs and he greeted my clitoris with his tongue.

"God..." I arched my back and gripped the sheets beside me, knowing this reality was better than any fantasy I'd ever had. He had the smoothest moves, and he was so sexy. I could have been doing this every night for years if I'd just opened my damn eyes.

He sucked my clit into his mouth then moved his tongue aggressively across the surface. Then he licked my opening before his tongue darted inside, greeting my wetness with his own. He didn't need to focus on the foreplay because I was already set to go. I'd been ready since I laid eyes on him in the bar.

I stared at him as he kept his face between my legs. My panties were hooked around my knees, and seeing him take me so aggressively almost made me come then and there. I wanted to release but I wanted to wait until he was inside me. There was no way I would last long, not after four months of no action.

After Zeke devoured me, he rose to his feet, his cock red and throbbing. He grabbed my dress and pulled it over my head, revealing my tits that were hard and pointed. He leaned over me and sucked each nipple into his mouth, his cock pressed against my soaked folds.

This had to be a dream. It was just too good.

I ran my hands through his hair just the way I wanted before I dragged my nails down his back, feeling every single line and groove of muscle. He was perfect, so masculine and strong. I closed my eyes and enjoyed all the sensations he created in me. Before he pulled away, he gave me a seductive kiss on the lips. He straightened, standing at the edge of the bed with his cock right against my folds.

I was on birth control and clean, and I knew Zeke was clean too. So I didn't need to have that conversation I had with Ryker when we became serious. It was different with Zeke, and I didn't want him to wear anything.

It was different with me too because he didn't open his nightstand and pull out a condom. He grabbed the base of his cock and pointed his thick head at my entrance.

"Wait… Do you think we should slow things down?" We just got together and we were jumping in bed together.

He stared at me with the same heated expression, like slowing down was the dumbest idea he'd ever heard. "If you want to."

"I don't. I just don't want you to think I'm a slut."

The corner of his mouth rose in a smile. "I don't think that, Rae. But I'm definitely going to turn you into a slut—for me." He pressed his head inside me, stretching me wide as he entered my narrow channel.

My head rolled back to the bed, and I gripped the sheets again. Everything I said came out in an incoherent blur. "Oh my god, that feels so fucking good."

He moved farther inside, his thick shaft pressing against my walls as he inched deeper. He glided through my slickness, feeling my arousal soak his skin. He kept going until every inch of his length was buried deep inside me.

"Zeke..." My hands moved to his wrists. I wrapped my fingers around his corded skin, feeling his powerful pulse through his weathered flesh. I hadn't felt this pleasure in so long I forgot how good it was. He was so big that it was a little painful, but that discomfort was nothing compared to how amazing he felt.

His eyes burned into mine as he listened to me say his name. "You don't know how many times I've beat off to just the idea of you saying my name like that." He pulled me closer to the edge, his cock moving just a little more. His hands moved to the back of my knees and he kept my thighs pinned apart.

"I want to watch you beat off sometime." I didn't have a clue what I was saying. My head was in the clouds and all I could think about was this sexy god inside me.

416

He started to move inside me, sliding through my slickness. His cock made noises every time it glided in and out, the friction audible.

I was already going to come. I knew it.

It was so pathetic that it was embarrassing.

I tried to fight it as he thrust into me gently. We hadn't even really started, and I was already fighting the fire between my legs. It started deep in my belly then migrated south. Like a crescendo, it rose until it was no longer unbreakable.

I came so hard I screamed.

"Oh god..."

Zeke's heated expression intensified as he stared at the pleasure on my face. He thrust into me harder, giving me every inch of his length at a quick pace to make the climax even more intense.

I dug my nails into his forearms and rocked my lower body against him, loving every single inch of that unbelievable cock. "Zeke...wow." I rode the high until it slowly disappeared from my body altogether, but I could still feel the tenderness from our moving bodies.

"You haven't seen anything yet, baby." He pulled his length out of me, making me feel empty the second he was gone. Then he scooted me up the bed and turned me on my stomach. He moved on top of me and shoved himself inside me harshly, not at all gently like he was before. He had me pinned underneath him, his chest against my back. His mouth moved to my ear and he fucked me aggressively, his hips smacking against my ass every time he pounded into me. My clit rubbed against the bunched-up sheets every time he moved into me, heightening the pleasure to a new level.

He breathed into my ear and grunted quietly, moving his entire body as he fucked me aggressively. He was covered in sweat, and when I rocked my ass back into him, I got drenched as well. It didn't matter how tired and hot we were. We were so lost in each other we didn't care about the heat. "Your pussy feels as good as I imagined."

I reached behind me and gripped him by the thigh, pulling him into me as I rocked into him. I could feel another orgasm approaching over the horizon, but I wasn't surprised because I was so hard up. "I can't wait until I feel your come inside me."

He paused for a second, a heavy breath filling my ear. "Fuck, Rae." He thrust into me harder, burrowing me into the mattress.

Hearing the desperation in his voice and feeling the increased hardness of his dick pushed me to the very edge. I came again, constricting around him like a snake around its prey. I squeezed him hard as my pussy sang, feeling such a high of pleasure I didn't think I would ever come down again.

It felt so damn good.

The best.

"Give it to me, Zeke."

He grunted against my ear and his strokes evened out, slowing in pace. Then he inserted himself completely inside me, balls deep. "Here it comes." His cock twitched inside me and he tensed noticeably, holding his breath as his tip exploded. "Fuck..." He continued to moan through the orgasm, depositing every drop of come deep inside me. "Fuck yeah." He buried his face in my neck as he caught his breath, our sweat mixing together. He kept his cock inside me as it slowly softened. Then he stayed there for a long time, recovering from what just happened.

"I'm sorry I came so quickly..." I was embarrassed by how easy it was to get me off. "I haven't been—"

"You'll always come quickly with me—and more than once."

***

When I opened my eyes the next morning, my head rested on Zeke's powerful chest. My arm was tucked around his hard waist, and his bare skin was warm to the touch. It took me a moment to realize this reality was true. I was truly naked in Zeke's bed, cuddling with him after a great night of sex and sleep.

I shifted in bed then looked up at him, seeing his heavy eyes look back at me. His arm was around my shoulder, and his large fingers moved up and down my side. He was sexy when he first woke up in the morning.

"Is this real?" I dreamed about this moment so many times I couldn't tell if it was just my imagination getting the best of me.

"Yeah." His fingers moved through my hair. "And if it's not, it's the best dream I've ever had." He turned on his side and cuddled with me, his face resting against my shoulder. The large windows in his bedroom led to his big backyard. A heavy fog had settled on the ground and blocked out visibility. The back fence couldn't even be seen. I wasn't sure what time it was, probably still early in the morning.

"You're a really good kisser," I blurted.

The corner of his mouth rose in a smile. "I hope you think I'm good at other things as well."

"Oh, I do," I said quickly. "I was just remembering our first kiss…"

"It's fun to think about, huh?" He kissed my shoulder, his soft lips so warm.

I didn't want to have this conversation, but I knew it had to happen. I'd been hurt too many times to make stupid assumptions. "So…was last night a one-night stand?" I couldn't keep the dread out of my voice. "It wasn't, right? Because—"

"I'm your man, Rae." He kissed my shoulder. "And you're my woman."

Relief entered my veins. "Well, there's something I should tell you. I don't want you to think this was just some compulsive, physical thing. A few months ago, I started to have feelings for you and they never went away…"

He stared at me like this information was redundant.

He wasn't surprised at that? At all? "Rochelle told me you used to have feelings for me. When I found that out, my feelings only became worse. The only reason why I didn't tell you was because you were seeing Rochelle at the time."

Still, nothing. "Rae, Rex told me everything about a month ago."

My heart plummeted into my stomach. My own brother betrayed me? He blabbed everything to Zeke? "What?"

"When he told me, it changed everything. Rochelle was great, and I was happy with her. But once you were in my mind, I couldn't get you out. I've wanted you for so long, and I couldn't miss the chance to have you. I never looked at Rochelle the same, and our relationship died in that instant. That was why I broke up with her."

"Because of me?" Now I really felt like shit. "I didn't want that to happen. That's why I never told you—"

423

"I know. But I'm glad I found out. This past month only assured me I made the right decision. Being with you is different. It's..." He tried to search for the right words. "It's like hanging out with your best friend and the hottest chick you've ever seen at the exact same time. Sometimes I wanted to kiss you, and other times, I couldn't stop laughing at something you said. This is where I belong."

His decision was in the past, and nothing we said now would change what happened. Rochelle was gone and their relationship was over for good. I could keep feeling bad about it, but it wouldn't change anything. "Why didn't you tell me?"

"I wanted to wait a while to get Rochelle out of my system. I know I made the right decision for leaving her, but I still cared about her and she was on my mind. I wanted to be alone for a while before I went for you—out of respect for both of you."

"Oh..."

"But when I saw the heartbroken look on your face when Theresa was talking to me, I knew I needed to come clean and stop dragging my feet."

"Who is she?"

"A patient."

I still didn't like her. She didn't need to grope her doctor's arm like that.

"So instead of telling you everything, I just kissed you instead. And that worked out pretty well."

Hell yeah, it did.

"So now we're here." He slowly rolled me to my back as his body covered mine. His muscular thighs separated mine and he leaned farther over me, his lips just inches from mine.

"Here we are..."

He pressed his head against my entrance, his large cock thick and throbbing.

I hooked my arms around his neck and stared deep into his eyes, feeling his length stretch me as it slid deeper inside. Sex had never felt so good, and my mind was in a haze of satisfaction.

Once he was completely inside me, he remained still, enjoying the feel of my wet pussy. He moaned quietly as he felt me stretch slowly, acclimating to his large size. Zeke was innately sexy, and he knew how to make all the right moves in bed. He was aggressive and authoritative, not always the gentleman he seemed to be—and I liked that.

I didn't see him as my friend anymore, and I hadn't in a long time. I saw him as the dreamiest hunk in the world, the man who owned my heart and every other part of my body. I felt safe with him like I didn't with anyone else. "You're so much better than my dreams."

He kissed the corner of my mouth as he moved deep inside me. "And you're so much better than my hand."

***

I walked through the door with Zeke behind me. It was Sunday night, and I had to go back to work the next day.

Unfortunately.

Rex was in the kitchen. He pulled a pizza pocket out of the microwave then gave us an uncomfortable look. "You're home…"

"Don't worry, I'm not staying." I was wearing the same dress and heels I'd been wearing on Friday night. I wasn't wearing any underwear because those were too old and too wet to wear now.

Saying this moment was awkward was an understatement.

"I'm just going to get some clothes and grab Safari." I walked down the hall, feeling guilty for leaving Zeke alone with Rex. It was undoubtedly awkward between them. But they had to get through it since they were best friends.

"How was your weekend?" Zeke asked.

I grabbed a bag and threw my clothes inside.

"It was alright," Rex said. "How was yours?"

"Good." That was all Zeke said.

Shit, it was tense.

"Hang out with Kayden?" Zeke asked.

"We went to the beach yesterday," Rex said. "Had a little picnic."

"That sounds nice," Zeke said.

"Yeah," Rex said. "It was cool."

I put a leash on Safari and then walked back into the entryway, saving Zeke from the tensest conversation on the planet. "I'm ready."

"When are you coming back?" Rex asked.

"When I run out of clothes," I said bluntly. I wasn't leaving Zeke's place until I absolutely had to. I didn't want to leave his side, or his bed, for even a moment. I wanted to wear his t-shirt around the house all day long with his boxers underneath. I wanted to see Safari run around in the backyard.

Zeke grabbed my bag and hung it over his shoulder. "Alright. We'll see you later."

Rex looked a little sick. "Okay…"

This awkwardness shouldn't even have been there. It was strange that it existed at all. "Rex, stop being weird. Zeke and I are sleeping together. It's not that ridiculous."

Rex took a bite out of his pizza pocket. "It'll just take some time to get used to. I thought this day would happen, but now that it has…it's just awkward."

"Well, get over it," I said. "Because this arrangement is going to last a really long time."

Zeke automatically smiled when he heard what I said. "You heard her. I'm gonna be around for a *long* time."

Rex rolled his eyes. "Just shut up and go."

Zeke took my hand and walked me outside. Safari was connected to the leash held in my hand, and since Zeke was there, he seemed to know where we were headed. Zeke eyed me with the same smile still on his face.

"What?"

"I like what you said back there."

"That this thing will last a long time?"

"Yeah."

"I wouldn't risk our friendship if I didn't think it could last forever."

He stopped walking and his smile disappeared. He stared me down like he didn't know what to say. "Yeah?"

"Yeah."

He nodded. "I think it's going to last forever too."

My heart stopped beating in my chest once those words were exchanged. We didn't make a commitment or even say we loved each other, but somehow, those words felt heavy. I didn't know where our relationship would go because we'd only been seeing each other for a few days, but deep in my gut, I knew it was special. I knew it was different from any other relationship I'd had before.

We didn't know what would be at the end of this road until we walked the path. But I was excited to find out where we would end up. Although there was one concern I had. "No matter what happens, we'll always be friends." I extended my hand so we could shake on it. "Because I couldn't live without you in my life."

He eyed my hand before he took it. "Of course."

"Promise?"

He nodded. "Promise."

A smile formed on my lips.

And he smiled back.

Ray of Love

The story continues in Book 4, Ray of Time.

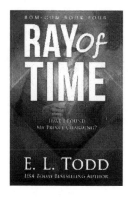

Dear Reader,

Thank you for reading Ray of Love. I hope you enjoyed reading it as much as I enjoyed writing it. If you could leave a short review, it would help me so much! Those reviews are the best kind of support you can give an author. Thank you!

Wishing you love,

E. L. Todd

Ray of Love

E. L. Todd

Want To Stalk Me?

Subscribe to my newsletter for updates on new releases, giveaways, and for my comical monthly newsletter. You'll get all the dirt you need to know. Sign up today.

www.eltoddbooks.com

Facebook:

https://www.facebook.com/ELTodd42

Twitter:

@E_L_Todd

Now you have no reason not to stalk me. You better get on that.

EL's Elites

I know I'm lucky enough to have super fans, you know, the kind that would dive off a cliff for you. They have my back through and through. They love my books, and they love spreading the word. Their biggest goal is to see me on the New York Times bestsellers list, and they'll stop at nothing to make it happen. While it's a lot of work, it's also a lot of fun. What better way to make friendships than to connect with people who love the same thing you do?

Are you one of these super fans?

If so, send a request to join the Facebook group. It's closed, so you'll have a hard time finding it without the link. Here it is:

https://www.facebook.com/groups/119232692 0784373

Hope to see you there, ELITE!

Made in the USA
Lexington, KY
29 January 2017